A Book with No Author

Brent Robison

Song lyrics quoted in the chapters "E.2 Terrible Tuesday" and "A New Friend" are copyright Eric Wood and are used by permission. They come from the following songs:
"Voodoo Wind" and "Close to the Bone" (*Letters from the Earth*, 1997)
"Frequency" and "Moonless Monday" (*Don't Just Dance*, 2001).
More information: http://ericwood.com/

Cover design by Bryan Maloney
Front cover photo and author photo by Wendy Drolma

Print ISBN: 979-8-9886702-0-9

Library of Congress Control Number: 2023948424

RECITAL PUBLISHING
Woodstock, NY
https://recitalpublishing.com

Recital Publishing is an imprint of the online podcast The Strange Recital
Fiction that questions the nature of reality
https://thestrangerecital.com

For the Gang of Six

.

Contents

"Things are not as they appear. Nor are they otherwise."
—Lankavatara Sutra

"How do you tell when you're out of invisible ink?"
—Steven Wright

Part I:

The Orphaned Manuscript

An Editorial Note

I, Brent Robison, am not the author of the fragmented story that follows. The manuscript arrived in my mailbox in Woodstock, New York, one day near the end of 2005. It was held together by two large clips that left rust marks on the pages. The thick stack of paper was wrapped in a plastic grocery bag inside a manila envelope with a Mississippi postmark, and was accompanied by a scrawled note that simply said:

Found this in the debris thought you probly want it, hard to find your new adress but finally did! So here it is, God bless.

There was no cover page nor title, just the words "Draft 1" in the top right corner of the first page. The irony is that the name in the opposite corner, presumably the author's name, was not mine, but nearly mine: "Brett Robinson." Subsequently, I spent over three years making an exhaustive search for the author. I followed every clue in the text but was not successful.

One more note: The final segment, labeled "To Whom It May Concern," was not part of the page-numbered typescript. It was a handwritten letter on a sheet torn from a yellow legal pad, clipped to the end of the manuscript. Its addition and cleanup, plus the removal of "Draft 1" and "Brett Robinson" for layout purposes, are my only editorial contributions.

What happened next, you'll find at the end of this book.

A. The Photographer

A.1 "Desert Vacation," a Short Story by Robbie Brand

THE SKY IS ONE shade of blue, horizon to horizon. It's glossy and hard, a vast overturned bowl of fine china baked to brilliant sapphire. Under it, a broken line of humans stretches long and thin across the flats, then bunches thick at steep places where footing is treacherous. Each silent hiker is one bone, one vertebra in the spine of a snake that winds its way over and around crag and boulder, skin against stone.

The pale young man walks in a daze. He is thin. He trudges through an oven, the ground glaring white under that hard sky. When a trickle of sweat starts down his forehead, it's gone in a second, sucked away by the dust-dry air. Up ahead, his even younger and paler wife limps between two men, her arms around their shoulders. He doesn't look at them.

"WHAT WE NEED IS a vacation together," he had said one night as they lay in darkness, staring at opposite walls.

She seemed small under the blankets, too small to be a wife and mother. He was exhausted and she was crying again, both of them battered by the wails of a six-month old, the midnight feedings, the walking, rocking, and more wails that lasted until mere minutes before the relentless morning alarm.

"A little communing with nature, that's it," he said. She didn't answer.

He searched the adventure brochures and finally convinced her to leave their daughter with Grandma and come on this three-day "survival experience" in the desert a few hours' drive from home. But he hadn't counted on a twist: her foot slammed hard against stone during a rappelling exercise in the early morning light.

"Thanks!" she had spit at him later as the group rested on the trail and she watched her toenail blacken. They hadn't spoken since.

HOURS PASS. A CRUEL blush has begun, faint pink on the young man's pasty forehead. He keeps his dry lips closed to protect his tongue from the air. He blindly sets one foot in front of the other, again and again. Then, gradually, he's aware of a whisper of moisture brushing his cheek, a sweet hint of green in his nostrils. It's the muddy San Rafael River, swirling in its channel a hundred feet below, between cliffs dark with mineral stains. The narrow trail skirts the cliff edge, then leads away, out of sight of the river, wandering through slabs of rippled slickrock and across dunes dotted with blade-clumps of yucca, and meanders down a long slope to come suddenly upon the river again, rolling brown at the hikers' feet. The San Rafael in late summer is no Mississippi. It's thirty feet wide, chest deep in the center channel, sluggish, sandy, cool but not cold.

Across the water, rust-streaked cliffs rise from a narrow beach to a jumbled slope of boulders that leads the eye up to a new set of hard cliffs, a blackish butte against the sky. This is Mexican Mountain, base camp.

The young wife immediately has her boot off and her foot in the water. She's grimacing. Her husband watches, then goes to her. "I'm sorry," he says.

She grabs his arm as she tries to stand, looking up at him with eyes that brim. "It just hurts so much. It's throbbing clear up to my head."

"I'm sorry," he says again, as if he knows no other words.

Holding his arm, she hobbles along the edge of the river to where the others are gathered near a lean-to that the guide has built against a sandstone overhang. The young man gently brushes his fingertips along the back of her hand as it rests on his arm. Her toenail is completely black, the toe purple and swollen. I want to kiss it, he thinks. More gently than is humanly possible, like the way air feels on your cheek, fanned by the wings of a dragonfly that's here then gone.

The hikers fan out, each searching a site for the required "solo" camp. The pale young couple make their way downstream, slowly, crippled, her arm around his neck. Inside a half-mile, they find the perfect spot, where a bend in the river has left a wide area of smooth sand surrounded by six-foot willows. Three old cottonwoods with their craggy bark and acid-green leaves stand twenty yards away. The San Rafael curves in sunshine, then slips in under the dark red cliffs on the other side, bending again in shadow and disappearing behind the stand of willows on its way to join the wider, muddier Green.

"I'm gonna cool off," she says. He looks for firewood while she strips and wades gingerly into the stream. He steals a glance at her. The sun hangs low; shadows are long. The air is alive with golden particles and the cliff above the river glows deep brilliant sienna. The stream slides by in shattered color, shards of mirror reflecting the orange cliff in wild patterns broken in ripples by the rich cobalt of the sky. Her body is silhouetted against the molten glare on the water. Her hands seem to be ladling gems as she splashes her sunburned shoulders, and clear droplets like liquid diamonds roll down her back. She turns slowly, nipples erect, skin roughened with goosebumps; golden light skims the tiny blond hairs of her thighs, then the fuller, darker tuft. She lowers herself into the water chin-deep, gasping just a little. The young man looks away, glancing here and there, picking up sticks of driftwood and dead sage branches, mindless of everything but the vision in the river. He looks again.

When she stands, the golden water streams down across her skin like summer rain on the smooth marble of an Aphrodite in some mythic ruin, and she wades toward him in slow motion, dripping. He's blind to her awkward limp.

Behind her the cliff wall shimmers in fluid patterns of light and the only sounds are a rustle of water against sand, a tiny gurgle of whirlpools under the willows, a faint whisper of a breeze in the cottonwoods. Slowly, he stands from stacking wood to face her as she steps from the water. He's stunned, he's crazy, he's in the presence of the sacred. It's as if, just maybe, he could be in love again. As if it's the night he first gazed at all of her, in moonlight, lying soft and open across the back seat of his car, a sweet wash of white skin like the foam of a wave in a sea of dark blue.

Now, in this wild place, in this bright slant of coppery sun, she seems to be smiling a little, softly, at him, like she did then. He steps to her, to hold her. As his hand rests lightly on her hip, she says, "Don't," and turns her back to him.

There is really no mistaking the absoluteness of her single word, but he refuses to believe it. He's her husband. He reaches around her from behind, his hands on her naked stomach, pulling her close, her wet skin cool against him.

In her ear, he murmurs, "Mmm, you feel so nice."

"Don't." This time the word is solid ice, an icicle dagger that hangs in the hot air, and she feels so cold he drops his arms to his sides. For one blind second, rage seethes up in him and he wants to throw her to the sand and pierce that cold shell again and again with stone-hard fury.

But he turns and walks stiffly to the river, drops his clothes and wades in, bending his knees till the cool current covers his shoulders and begins to sweep away the pain inside his skin.

The western sky beyond the cottonwoods blazes in ripples of pink and orange against turquoise, and around his sunburned face is a rolling glass reflection of the sky. He watches his wife dress, rimmed by sunlight catching the fine gold hair on her body, and he thinks of the moist softness of her lips, the salt and sweet taste of her, the breathy sighs and whispers in his ear as stomachs meet in a slippery film of sweat, the pink warmth engulfing them in sudden gasps, and the long slow touching afterward as the sky deepens to aquamarine. In the desert stream, he reaches down and grasps himself, and the silty flow caresses him, envelopes him, every inch of him, like the touch of an endless feather, tender but insistent, pulling, growing more urgent, and he's angry and he's sad as he thinks of her and what they won't have tonight, and he loves her and he hates her, and he shudders, sending his fluids swirling down the stream, to carry on through forty miles of desolation to where the San Rafael meets the Green, and on fifty more miles to mix with the Colorado in the tangled stone heart of Canyonlands, and on and on to fade into the parched lands of Mexican farmers, never ever finding the sea.

He climbs out of the water as the sun slips behind the hills, and suddenly everything is blue and gray under fading coral, and a cooling breeze stirs the willows. Silently, he dresses. She limps as they both gather wood, build a fire, and put together a simple dinner of ash cakes and dehydrated soup, speaking only for necessities.

They chew and think, their eyes don't meet, and the sky grows dark, splashed with bright stars. They sit cross-legged in an eerie circle of dancing orange shadows, while around them the blackness seems to have made this vast landscape shrink to a tiny space around their fire.

Something is crawling into the flickering light near the young man's feet. Just an inch long, a cruel white hook on slow spindly legs, it strolls uncaring across their sandy dinner table. The long shadow of its up-curled stinger leaps across the ridges of sand like a crazed warrior as its oddly-jointed legs scissor mechanically along. It's a scorpion, the deadly sort, the fierce kind that with one strike of an upturned tail could make this little desert trip a dark disaster, a morbid memory of desperation and pain, perhaps an ending, an ending of everything.

When he glances at his wife, her eyes are staring, fixed on the thing. It seems like a ghost in the dim mad dance of light. He's not sure it's really there. He blinks and it seems there, then gone, then there again, pale and mean.

Very slowly, he reaches for the aluminum pan from the mess kit at his side. With a whoop, he smashes the flat of the pan down hard on the thing, crushing it into the sand, twisting the pan, pushing till he's sure it's flattened and dead. He holds the pan there a long time.

When he lifts the pan up, there is nothing under it.

He's suddenly up on his knees, looking all around the flame-lit circle, straining his eyes to see a tiny rabid phantom scuttling furiously across the ground. Nothing. He picks up a stick and probes into the sand where the dead thing should be. Nothing. He digs more frantically, stirring the sand thoroughly all over the area, around the fire, under him, everywhere. Still nothing. Insane, shouting, he shakes their blankets, he scatters their pans and cups and food and clothes into the darkness. But no tiny monster is there, nothing is there, nothing.

He sits again. He looks at this pale young woman, his wife. Her eyes meet his, childlike, wide with terror. They go on sitting there, the two of them, in the wild flicker of the fire, under the hard black bulk of cliffs standing against deep blue and the silver dust of stars, silent, inert, on and on into the night.

A.2 An Impossibility

A.J. Campbell lowered the folded newsprint to his lap. His heart fishtailed and he struggled to breathe. This thing he had just read was an impossibility.

Afternoon sunlight continued to stream down on him as he sat on the bench in the median. The aroma of fresh bagels wafted from the backpack at his side, but he no longer noticed. Cars and people kept on moving past, but the cacophony of New York City had gone silent. A.J. wrestled with his stubborn mind, straining for a ray of understanding.

Twenty minutes earlier, after picking up a dozen of the city's best bagels from H&H, he had stopped at the corner of Broadway and 80th and grabbed a half-tabloid size publication from a rack on the sidewalk. It was a free paper that had suddenly started appearing all over Manhattan, the inaugural issue—Spring 1994—of *Espresso Lit*. He had set down his bag and relaxed on a bench in the tree-lined strip between the lanes of Broadway traffic, happy to be lounging in the perfect June sunshine. He had perused the pages, read a six-line poem, glanced at the first sentences of an essay or two, then settled in to read a piece under the Fiction heading whose title had caught his eye. It was a short story called "Desert Vacation," written by someone named Robbie Brand.

But it was A.J.'s story. It was an episode from his own life, from nearly ten years ago, and it had things in it that no one knew, not even his ex. They were secrets, his alone.

After a moment of mute grappling, his stunned inner silence gave way to a deluge of questions and curses. Could this be a coincidence? Could someone have had the very same experiences that he had? Could a writer have imagined scenes identical to his own life?

No, no, and no.

Then, goddamn it, who is this Robbie Brand guy? And how the fuck did he get my story?

A.J. was afraid he knew at least part of the answer. During the year of his divorce and career change—months that were both terrible and wonderful—he had formed a habit of scribbling in notebooks: his thoughts, the events of his life. He had kept at it for the four years since and had begun to enjoy the writing process. So, the problem was that he had written this very story himself—or a version of it, a rather different version—first in his journal, then typed up, in manuscript form. His somewhat vague artistic goal was to get it published as a "personal photo essay" or some such thing, in which his photographs of the desert would illustrate his "memoir." Or the text would be captions for a coffee-table photo book. Or something.

The text was printed up and ready to go, with taglines inserted for where the images should go. But then he'd had second thoughts. He was no writer, he was a photographer only—a picture-guy, not a word-guy. Not only that, but the "truth" he told made him look like a jerk—which, sometimes, he was. So he chickened out and left the stack of pages hidden in a desk drawer in his apartment. It had been there for several months now.

The fact that the setting, the characters, the sequence of events, had all been set to paper—had been brought forth from his mind into physical reality—told him that there was only one way this could have happened. Someone, probably someone he knew, had read his journal or his manuscript. Then had rewritten it and published it under a pseudonym. The creep had stolen his work. The creep had stolen his life.

But how? And who? And, perhaps inconsequentially, why?

The last question could be answered rather easily: Why? Because they could. That was human nature.

The other questions A.J. vowed to answer. Awareness of his surroundings returned all at once as an ambulance blasted past with an ear-splitting wail. He was on his feet, heading for the bank of phones that stood on the uptown side of 80th.

The number for *Espresso Lit* was in the small print of the masthead. His quarter clinked into the phone. As it rang, he eyed the headlines in the row of newspaper vending machines along the curb: the President defending himself against accusations of sexual harassment. Who's lying, Bill Clinton or Paula Jones?

Right. Everybody's lying, that's who.

A woman answered. "I need some information about one of the authors published in your new issue," A.J. said. "Can you help me with that?"

"The only information I can give you is what's printed on the back page in the contributors' notes. Did you look there?" She sounded pleasant, but bored.

"Oh." A.J. flipped the paper over and found the name in bold type. But he saw with a glance the blurb was useless:

Robbie Brand *likes his martinis shaken, not stirred. He may give up the writing racket at any moment.*

"This guy Robbie Brand—there's no information here. The guy stole my story. I need to talk to him."

"You're referring to, um, 'Desert Vacation,' right? Are you saying the story was plagiarized? Because that's a serious accusation."

"Look, I don't know about any legal definitions or anything. I didn't write these exact words, no. But this is my story, from my life. I don't know how he got it, but it's not cool. Not cool at all."

"Okay..." Her voice went soft and sweet. "It couldn't be just a marvelous parallel? Or that you feel a real kinship with the characters? I mean, that's what a fiction writer does, sir, if you know what I mean."

"Yeah, you think I'm a wacko. I'm not. Can you put your boss on the phone?"

Her sugary tone vanished. "Ha. I *am* the boss. I'm the editor. There are only two of us who run this thing, it's part-time, you were lucky to catch me in. And I need to tell you: each of our authors signs a contract stating that they have full ownership of the material they submit to us, so *Espresso Lit* is definitely not liable."

"Okay, okay, I don't intend to sue you or anything. I just want to talk to this Robbie Brand guy. And maybe you should, too."

"Like I said, I can't give you any information."

"But didn't you pay him? You must have his address or something."

She took a deep breath and exhaled into his ear. "I'm sorry. The best I can do is take your name and number and let him know that you need to speak to him. Will that suffice?"

"That'll be helpful, thanks." A.J. calculated that he had planted a seed of suspicion in her mind, so she would indeed contact Brand, and there was a chance she would give him A.J.'s contact information. But at the same time, he assumed Brand (whoever he really was) didn't need that information. After all, there was a distinct possibility he'd already been in A.J.'s apartment. He'd already snooped through A.J.'s private things, read his journal, touched every surface with his greasy, contaminated fingers. So the call would work to serve him notice: he'd been found out. The bastard couldn't hide forever.

A.J. headed east on 80th. He was on his way to the day's work, a cameraman gig at 89th and Central Park West. There were few things he loved more than striding through the streets of New York on a beautiful day, and usually he would marvel at the unlikely fact of himself, a bumpkin from rural Utah, at home in the world's greatest city. But today the brownstones and blossoms and noisy bustle disappeared under a chaos of thought. His memory was like a lightbox covered with color slides, as if the moments of his early marriage, its nasty end, his new life, were gathered into one simultaneous reality, a jumble of hues and moods all present at once.

One memory rose to the surface, floating on the feeling of inexplicable mystery he'd felt ever since he read the story in *Espresso Lit.* A few years earlier, he'd had an encounter with a stranger in a diner, a homeless hitchhiker who had seemed to wield some sort of hypnotic power over him. The man had seemed to be in two places at once, sitting with A.J. while also apparently rescuing a waitress from a criminal assault. Then he disappeared. A.J. had never been able to answer to his own satisfaction just what had happened that night, but he hadn't been hurt in any way. In fact, the guy had been something of an inspiration, a gentle shove that sent A.J. toward a bold career change, a redefinition of himself, at the very time that his marriage was falling apart. But the whole thing had left A.J. with the conviction that there were things in this world that could not be explained. And now, that vibration was abuzz in his cells again: under his anger lived a strange fascination with the very impossibility of the situation he found himself in.

He loved the enigma, but at the same time, *goddamn it*, he wanted an answer. He visualized himself as a detective, tracking down clues until everything made sense. A temporary identity: private investigator on his own case. So that would be his next endeavor, he decided. Or rather, he would fit it in somehow, third priority after making a living and spending time with his kids.

He kept a steady pace, not so fast as to raise a sweat, picking his route on the fly by the red or green lights at every corner, never breaking stride: east on 80th, up Amsterdam to 82nd, then east again; up Columbus to 84th, then east again, and up Central Park West to his destination. He arrived a few minutes before the call time of 2:00 and found the production van already at the curb. Along with the video engineer and the second cameraman, A.J. loaded cases of gear onto two rolling carts and strapped them down with bungees. More crew members arrived and as the other cameraman left to park the van, the crew wheeled their carts to the service entrance of the stately pre-war building and took the elevator to the fifth floor.

This job was one of many that A.J. had worked on for Image Impact Incorporated, I.I.I., a small husband-wife production company that served various corporate and educational clients. He always liked getting called by them; typically, the projects were not very exciting but they paid fairly and on time, and the crew, a handful of freelancers like himself, had become his friends. A.J. felt fortunate that, although he was a relative newcomer to the business, he had recently moved into a senior camera/lighting role with this company.

The shooting location was the high-ceilinged home office of a doctor who was the head of the addiction psychiatry department at NYU. They would be taping him in an interview with another

specialist in addiction treatment. The location was familiar since
the crew had shot other segments of this educational series in the
same space. But the setup was not easy, a three-camera arrangement
in a room that, while spacious, was not meant for all that gear and
had tall windows whose light had to be controlled.

Everybody went straight to work, but the banter never stopped.
They all kidded each other as tripods went up, cameras clicked
onto fluid heads, cables were strung, lights were raised on stands,
barndoors adjusted and diffusion attached, microphones tested.
A.J. had always loved the teamwork, but today he felt removed,
in an invisible bubble of isolation. He kept up a cheerful front
to cover a creeping distrust. Could any of these people be Robbie
Brand? As far as he knew, none of them aspired to be a writer. But
how could he be sure? From the President on down, no one was
really who they seemed.

When setup was finished, the two doctors took their seats in
front of the cameras as microphones were clipped to their ties and
final tweaks were made to hair, makeup, lighting. The "Roll tape!"
command was given and A.J. was able to enter the zone, the mental
space that he always enjoyed on a job like this. It was a sort of
fully-engaged relaxation, maintaining a laser-like concentration on
the focus and framing of the shot in his viewfinder while at the
same time calmly listening to everything the subjects were saying.

Today's discussion was about the value of Alcoholics Anonymous and its spinoff, Narcotics Anonymous, as tools in the psychiatric treatment of addicts. The doctors were in full agreement
that the AA/NA program was an indispensable aid in their work.
Besides the fact that it provided the struggling addict with a com-
munity of fellow travelers plus a "sponsor" for individual support,
the philosophies embodied in the Twelve Steps were fully in sync

with current "best practices" for addiction psychotherapy. The "higher power" that was such an important part of the steps did not have to be the "God" defined by mainstream religion; it could mean each AA or NA group itself, the Twelve-Step program as a whole, or even the psychiatric treatment plan, for those few addicts who elected to go that route. The essential components were the addict's admission of his life's unmanageability and the surrender of his own obviously faulty will to something greater than himself, something with his genuine best interests in mind.

As A.J. watched and listened, his fingers lightly on the camera controls, the mystery that had been tormenting him faded out of his awareness. This was all new and fascinating information. Not because he had a substance abuse problem; he occasionally drank a beer or a glass of wine, and even more infrequently, shared a joint with friends. That was all; he could take it or leave it. But the discussion about the redefinition of God...there was a topic that piqued his interest. The trappings of his ultra-religious Mormon childhood—the irrational dogmas, the scripture quoting, the multiple prayers daily—all that was in the past now, left behind with his rejected former selves. But where did that leave God? A.J. wasn't buying that old image of a white-bearded father in the sky anymore, but...what instead? Something in him rebelled against the glib cliché, "you can take the boy out of the church, but you can't take the church out of the boy." And his encounter with the hobo hypnotist in the diner had pointed him toward new ways of seeing. He was determined that, eventually, whatever it took, he would be reborn into some deeper understanding of the invisible truths behind the video screen of the world. *I swear to God*, he thought with a smile.

The wrap went much faster than the setup. The sound man, Nick Pappas—tattooed, black-clad, always gruff—was working near A.J. and he spoke to no one in particular, "That was right on, what they said. You gotta surrender or you'll never kick."

A.J. said, "Yeah? Personal experience?"

Nick just kept coiling cables without looking up. "Sober seven years now. Still going to meetings. But that's the main thing—the idea that you're in control, it's just drunken arrogance. None of us are in control of anything. Something out there is taking care of it all, and it isn't you or me."

"Higher power, eh?"

"Damn right."

"Nick, you're a man full of surprises," A.J. said. "I never would have guessed. Congrats on your seven years." For a moment he felt strangely moved, as if tears might well up. But he'd been reminded of the unknowability of people, and a dull rage flared again. He worked in silence until it was time to head out into the fresh spring evening, toward home.

In the crowded subway downtown, A.J. stood, grasping a pole and staring down at everyone's shoes. His mind chewed on the feeling of being invaded—his story stolen. As anger faded to the background, he began to feel sick. Sometimes the sensation of being completely ineffectual in the world came over him like a dark blanket, and now it was here again, only this time mixed with something new: the added dimension that he had been unable to protect himself from intrusion. His boundaries had been encroached and he'd been utterly defenseless. What kind of man was he?

The studio apartment where he'd lived for three years, subletting from a friend of a friend, was cramped and old. It was two flights up on a blessedly quiet block, Jones Street just above Bleecker. A.J. entered with every sense alert, moving stealthily as if to avoid waking someone. But he lived alone; there was no one to awaken. He closed the door behind him and stood still, hoping to catch some subtle feeling; to see, smell, hear something, some evidence of an intruder. Nothing.

A.J. set his backpack on the floor and went directly to his desk. The manuscript of "Learning to Survive" was still there in the second drawer, looking entirely untouched. He picked it up and leafed through the pages. He brought it to his nose and sniffed. He placed an open hand on one of the smooth white sheets and closed his eyes. There was nothing—no scent, no vibration—nothing to indicate another human being had ever touched or even read these pages.

On a shelf above the desk, in a row, were his journals, different sizes and styles of books, a half-dozen volumes representing the last four years. They appeared to be exactly as he remembered, no fraction of an inch difference in their placement, no half-degree deviation in their angle of lean. Even the faint layer of dust on their top surfaces looked undisturbed. He selected a black-bound sketchbook and found the pages that held his original scribbles of what had eventually become "Learning to Survive," the private story some thieving impostor had transformed into "Desert Vacation."

As he stared at his own handwriting, A.J. realized: no one had been here, nothing had been taken nor even touched. There was a profound feeling of solitude and isolation in this room. No human but himself had entered this space in months. It was a tomb. An enormous wave of loneliness rolled over him. He wanted only to sleep. He replaced the book, slogged five heavy steps to his bed, and fell like a log onto its rumpled cover.

A.3 "Learning to Survive," a Photo Memoir by A.J. Campbell

[IMAGE: 1-08 Red cliff, blue sky]
I WAS FEELING GOOD that day, good and wild. Back then, it was always like that when I got out there in the wide-open wilderness. As though with each breath, I was breathing in Life—getting more alive, more awake, more aware. Every sight was beautiful, every sound musical, every smell fantastic perfume, every touch and taste urgent, exotic, exquisite.

So that's how I was feeling, and it was becoming a sexual thing. I looked at Molly. I felt crazy in love with her, as she stood there with me at the edge of that cliff, under that big blue sky.

It was a hot morning. Only eight, but hot already. We stood at the rim of a cliff, a long, ragged escarpment, sixty feet of vertical sandstone to the scrubby sage below. A pillar of sandstone stood separate like a giant splinter, split off, eroded from the bulk of the cliff, its crown a rough, rounded surface maybe ten by ten. Our first task was to jump from where we stood, the mainland, to that island. Just a four-foot leap, but below us was nothing—nothing but air, and then, far down in narrow shadows: cracked boulders, cactus, snakes.

[IMAGE: 1-23 Boulders-cactus]

Our second task, once each of us made the jump, was to rappel down the pillar. Dangle alone on a rope against the gritty, beautiful, pink sandstone in the hard morning sun, inching or plummeting according to individual style, down down to the welcome flat earth and congratulations from the group. I say "dangle alone" because that's the feeling you get. The actual truth is that nobody's alone. Like the brochure said, this was a carefully supervised Desert Survival Experience, with leaders at top and bottom "on belay," securing the rope, cool with instructions, warm with encouragement.

The twelve of us had left town in pre-dawn darkness, caravanning to a spot a mile from there, where the rutted road ended at a dry creek bed. A whole weekend of freedom was ahead for Molly and me. Freedom from uptight bosses, laundry, dirty dishes, car repair, and a cute ten-month-old baby girl who would cry every time we tried to make love. We had dropped her off at Grandma's, my mother's, so that Molly and I could have the weekend together.

And Mol was looking sexy as hell. It was all I could do to keep my hands off her, there with people all around. I wanted to taste that fine mist of sweat on her upper lip. I wanted to run my finger down her smooth throat, down the moist furrow between her pale small breasts that had grown bigger with motherhood, pushing against her t-shirt. Run my hand up her tan thigh, feeling delicate all-but-invisible downy gold, up to where the ragged edge of cut-off jeans hid paler skin, darker hair, softness so sweet I'm in pain, remembering. I liked the way she tossed her long blond braid, impatient to move ahead. Her hiking boots were small, like a child's. She was only nineteen.

[IMAGE: 1-30 Hand on rope]

Against advice, we all sneaked a peek into the crevice below. Then Mol and I waited our turn. Each person ahead of us would fret, falter, gather courage, run and jump, then slowly stand straight, stark against blue, as if on a peninsula in the sky. Helped by George, the guide, each would wind a heavy rope over a shoulder and around a thigh. Each would fret again, then walk slowly backward, disappearing below the rim of the rock, eyes wide.

It seemed that everyone but me was afraid. What I felt was a type of wild joy, as if that burning blue sky was running liquid in my veins. Then it was my turn. No hesitation: run, jump, land surefooted, stand, smile.

Molly resented that. "Oh, great, he makes everybody look chicken," she said.

She started her approach; ran a few steps. Her eyes blinked wide and she stopped. "Shit. Jimmy...." She looked at me. It was strange. First her eyes showed blind panic, then they pleaded. Then, all within a second, they sparked icy hatred. At me. This happened a lot. I never had time to respond to one thing before she was on to the next.

She backed up, took a deep breath, ran, and jumped. She did just fine, but there's always something, some random little misfortune. She landed with the toe of her right boot stubbed straight into the sloping stone.

"Ouch. Damn." She looked back at the gap she'd just flown over, then up at me, defiantly. "So there," she said, as if there was something at issue between us, which there wasn't. At least not to me.

"I knew you could do it," I said, giving her a paternal hug. "But on we go." Rope in hand, I put on a confident grin while my heart pounded. It wasn't fear exactly; more like that giddy feeling that made me giggle hysterically when I was a kid, pounding desperately through the orchard at twilight, my pockets full of stolen apples and Ol' Man Dodd shouting behind me.

I backed off the cliff, rope sliding through my hands, heating my thigh through my jeans as I slithered down, kicking off the wall once, twice, feeling free and tiny in a giant space, then hitting sandy earth.

[IMAGE: 1-15 M on rappel]

Mol came behind me, sluggish with fear, but finally down and proud of herself. I knew she was, although she tried not to show it. Then there was hugging, laughing, backslapping all around. She shrugged it off, trying to appear always tough and competent.

I could always see through that act of hers. I thought of myself as a lot older, though I was only twenty-two then. Plus, I was the very first person in my family, both sides, to go to college. Molly never even finished high school. And another thing: that desert was my kind of country, like the landscape of my imagination. She had never been there before. She mostly knew beaches, freeways, malls, pastel adobe subdivisions, all that Southern California stuff that drove me nuts. But I was sure she'd learn to like it out there in the desert. I believed love had that kind of power.

The main thing we did on that trip was walk. Walk, walk, under the cliffs, across the dunes, toward the campsite up ahead along the San Rafael River. It seemed like the trek took on a life, a rhythm, all its own. We went single file, mostly silent, the order gradually adjusting itself like natural selection. Some would fall behind, others move ahead, ebb and flow.

[IMAGE: 2-03 Line of hikers 1]

It was walking as meditation, a steady pace fast enough to force clarity of mind, picking each step among stones and sage, yet slow enough to permit communion with each new view, each new sensation of foot on earth, each angle of light, each shape and texture that rises up and is gone like driftwood down a river. I was in my element, the land of my soul. I walked, swinging along in an easy rhythm under the brassy sun, dreaming like I've dreamed out there since I was a child, like I still dream today. I was a mountain man, a Spanish explorer, a cavalry scout; I felt someone watching me, and with a chill down my spine, I saw a line of feathered heads and war-painted faces appear one at a time above the ledges on my right. Eyes fierce as eagles cut into me. I stared back, boldly.

Then my eyes landed on Molly's blue-jeaned roundness as she walked in front of me, and dreams of ancient warriors were gone like smoke in a breeze and I was right there in the now, lusting.

She was dressed like that when I first saw her, two years earlier, standing by the highway outside Barstow, hitching toward Vegas. She was a seventeen-year-old runaway looking for desperate anonymity in the capital of sleaze. I was on my way home after breaking up with my first college girlfriend, who lived in Pasadena.

Molly was a little shy when she got in my car, but cruising down a long highway can always make you relax and feel great. Pretty soon we smiled and joked and stole little glances at each other. Less than an hour after I'd picked her up, I knew I didn't want to let her go, so when she fell asleep, I flew right on past Vegas, not stopping until the needle hit empty at Pintura, Utah.

When she woke up, I got my first glimpse of her anger. Dark scowl, flushed face, hair flying, she called me foul names and kicked the dashboard. At first I was shocked because nobody in my family yelled like that. Anger wasn't allowed. But when she started to get out of the car, I grabbed her hand.

"You were so beautiful sleeping, so perfect and peaceful, I just wanted you to stay with me forever," I said, then I kissed her. It worked.

We drove on to my folks' place in Richfield, where I was staying for summer break after my sophomore year at the "U" up north. Mol stayed in an extra room at my friend's house and got a job at McDonalds. We were together every day. That was one wild, sexy summer.

[IMAGE: 2-13 Hikers at rest]

I noticed Molly was walking slower. In fact, we were the last people in line. The others were out of sight. Quietly, I moved up close behind her, caressed her arm and whispered in her ear, "I think we're alone now..." like the old Tommy James song. It was one of our jokes. She violently pulled her arm away, and as she did, I glimpsed tears in her eyes, a red face, jaw clenched. I was stunned, like the time I got hit in the nose by a baseball. I dropped back without a word, but then I noticed she was limping.

"What's wrong?"

"Just leave me alone."

"Why are you limping?"

"Go away."

"Blisters? I think George has some moleskin."

"Just shut up and leave me alone. And thanks a lot." She said this with a little snort of breath. I couldn't tell if it was from pain or just simple meanness.

I really hated this. What the hell did I do? It got all complicated in my head. Partly there was anger, like—right, sure, whatever is wrong with her foot is my fault, just like everything that goes bad in her life. But there was also a sort of sadness and I started to look back on everything to find where I screwed up. I couldn't find it, so I decided to be angry.

I dropped back ten yards behind her, then we rounded a bend in the trail and came upon the rest of the group. Everyone had stopped to rest, taking gulps from canteens, savoring thin patches of shade behind man-high boulders and scraggly junipers. Mol fumbled off her boot and sock and I saw her toenail was ugly purple.

People gathered around, oohing and aahing. Somebody said, "Is it broken?" Somebody else said, "Nah, but she'll lose that nail for sure." Another one said, "I doubt it. I had one looked worse'n that, healed up fine."

Molly snapped, "Look, the problem is I can't walk anymore, so I could care less if I lose the damned nail!"

People murmured. "Maybe it *is* broken," somebody said.

"You mean you *couldn't* care less," I said, with a little laugh. "The correct form of that expression is *couldn't* care less."

Everybody was silent. I licked my dry lips.

"I mean, look at it this way." I glanced around at the others to make my point. "If you don't care at all, zero, you couldn't care any less, right? But if you said you *could* care less, that means you must care a little, right?" I looked at Mol. "And that's not really what you meant to say."

Teary and red-faced, she glared at the ground. The air was bright and hard. The heat made everything still, as if there was no breathing allowed. The only sound I heard was the strange electric buzzing of a cicada in one of the junipers across the dry wash. Somebody stirred.

"What's this?" Clark and George, the leaders, broke through the group. "Ooh, looks painful," Clark said as they both knelt. "You must have been hurting for a while. Brave lady."

George's fingers touched quickly here and there, then he said, "Well, I don't think it's broken, but let's keep you off that foot as much as we can. Jimmy, you wanna take one side, Todd, you take the other?"

I stepped up to put her arm over my shoulder when she turned away. "Don't touch me," she said.

I just stood there, feeling stupid. People looked at the ground, shuffled toward the trail, threw quick glances at Molly. Todd, the big soft blonde who never spoke, had one of her arms, then Kenny, a tall skinny kid with a prominent Adam's apple, took her other. They started down the trail ahead of me. Their arms were around her waist, hers around their shoulders.

I felt miserable. The heat seemed unbearable as I swung back into the rhythm of the trail, staring at the ground passing by under my feet. I thought of black desert nights, rough hands chipping flint into cruel arrowheads in the demented flicker of a sagebrush fire.

[IMAGE: 2-26 M between T and K]

When Molly had realized she was pregnant, she bristled with blame, red-faced and full of ugly accusations. Then she crumpled into tearful hysteria as we sat in my car on a desolate country road, crying, planning, fighting, laughing, crying, holding each other until the sky turned pearly gray and she was needed to serve Egg McMuffins at the drive-up. I told her I'd take care of her. I knew I could.

I'm from a small town, a big clan of Mormons. We believed in marrying young, getting a family started early. This was a good thing, I said to everyone. My dreams of being a photographer, maybe even a filmmaker, could wait; family is more important. My mom and stepdad saw it that way too, or so they said. My two younger sisters were excited to have a sister-in-law, a niece or nephew coming soon.

Molly's mom wasn't so sure. To break the news, we made a short visit back to Mol's home, a cookie-cut adobe ranch house in a generic suburb. Her little brother and sister immediately hounded us with questions. We laughed, we chatted, but then we got serious. Her mom, tired-looking but surprisingly young because she'd been a teenage mother herself, protested such a hasty marriage—protested lamely, for two minutes, then gave in. About the baby, there were no congratulations. In fact, I sensed behind her apathy a subtle gloating: her daughter was no better than she had been. I was secretly shocked by all this parental abdication; I felt sorry for Molly. In the end, I think her mother was just glad to get rid of her.

[IMAGE: 2-35 Line of hikers 2]

We were hiking in a long, broken line, everyone tired and silent. I felt eyes upon me from the cliffs above the trail, the eyes of dark-skinned people long dead, not movie Apaches, but the truly Ancient Ones. Where the canyon walls narrowed, I heard whispering, faint echoes in a strange guttural tongue, strange but familiar, that spoke not in words but in images and inner twinges in the tissue. I drifted, somewhere into memory like wisps of dream. I thought, these things are mine, these are the traces left by me—these chipped flint arrowheads, these blackened fire holes, these shards of finely crafted pots, these strange sketches of beasts and gods scratched in stone high on cliff walls.

[IMAGE: 3-02 Petroglyph]

I was trudging through an oven, glaring white under that hard sky. When a trickle of sweat started down my forehead, it was gone in a second, evaporated, sucked away by the dust-dry air. Sunburned, crusty, squinting, a man in the desert, a boy in heaven, a boy in his own godforsaken land.

Two hours later, the trail ran along the edge of a narrow canyon where cliffs dark with mineral stains dropped below our feet to the muddy San Rafael River. I saw myself suddenly on the other side of this chasm, alone, unable to reach the group. And Mol walked along with them, glancing indifferently across the space at me. I imagined her walking on her own now, strongly, her tan thighs glistening and stray strands of her golden hair floating. She led them. I was stopped by a rattlesnake in the trail, but they continued, out of sight, and I was stuck, immobile, numb. I was snake-bit, abandoned. Dead. I wished I was dead.

But I was still there, behind the group. They'd stopped to rest again, sprawled and heaped randomly about, silent, raising dusty canteens to cracked lips. I came up close to Molly and said quietly, "Why is it always my fault when something is wrong?"

She looked sad. "I miss my baby," she said.

"I know," I said, then I put my hand on her cheek. It felt so nice to touch her. She let it stay there a moment, then her brows pinched darkly, that familiar storm cloud.

"You love to humiliate me, don't you?" Her voice was a hiss, her eyes slits. She turned and limped away, putting on a bright cheery face as she playfully punched Clark in the shoulder and said, "Hey, are we lost yet? How much further to camp?"

[IMAGE: 3-11 Dusty boots]

With everyone on the move again, I maneuvered to where I was walking with Clark, because I needed to talk to him about the night's sleeping arrangements. I knew that when we reached our base camp, it was time for "solo." Everybody would split up to spend the night alone, spread out along the river at quarter-mile intervals. I had other ideas.

Clark was the vocational rehab counselor whose agency sponsored the excursion. It was meant as therapy for his clients—mostly people struggling with alcohol and drug problems who can't keep a job. I had consulted him about how to get back to school after dropping out, getting married, having a kid. But I was sure I was not like the rest of those losers. Molly and I were on that trip because Clark lived in our neighborhood. We were friends, and I was counting on that to get him to make an exception to the rules.

"But Clark, y'know, Mol and I haven't had any time alone since the baby was born. The reason we came on this trip was to be together, not to spend the night apart."

"I can understand that," Clark said. "My problem is, everybody else goes solo; they wonder why you get special treatment. And you know, I think it would be good for both of you to do a solo tonight. Tomorrow night you can be together."

"That's just not the reason we came though, Clark."

"Maybe you should schedule a night in a hotel when you get back to town."

He was older, maybe mid-thirties. I'd heard he had marital problems, so I hoped he'd understand. "It's just not the same. And anyway, if you put us in separate spots, we'll just get together anyway. I mean, come on, what's the point?"

"Well, have it your way," he said with a sigh. "I guess you know best what you need out of this trip."

"Thanks, man."

[IMAGE: 3-23 San Rafael R.]

After a couple more miles of meandering through sandstone slabs and drifted dunes, the trail brought us suddenly to the bank of the river. The San Rafael was not a big river, nor a fast one. Its sandy brown current lazed past our feet. On the other side, cliffs and boulders leapt up to a dark hulk, Mexican Mountain. No sooner had we heard that this was our destination, than Molly had her bare foot in the water.

"I'm sorry," I told her. She blinked back tears and groaned in pain. Her toenail was black, the toe swollen. I wanted to make it better but felt totally helpless. All I could say was "I'm sorry" again.

She held my arm as we hobbled along the riverbank to where the others were gathered around a makeshift shelter that George had built on a previous visit. Clark and George explained the solo idea to everybody and made plans for the following night to be a fun reunion around a big bonfire, with campfire songs and all. They took the group upriver to begin locating campsites, but Mol and I went downstream. We limped and hopped, her arm around my neck, until we found a wide sandy bank guarded by tall willows, with a stand of gnarly old cottonwoods nearby. The river glinted in sunshine on our side but looked cool and dark in the shadow of the vertical bronze cliffs across the water.

[IMAGE: 3-32 Water reflections]

As I began picking up driftwood for a fire, Molly dropped her clothes on the ground and waded carefully into the stream. The sun was low and its light slanted across the water, rimming her naked body with a golden glow. She splashed water like diamonds over her shoulders, and I couldn't keep my eyes off her body, those sweet, perfect curves of flesh both soft and firm. In that moment, she seemed like a goddess, a vision of primal beauty from another age. All our discomfort, even her limp as she waded back toward me, seemed to disappear, and I was consumed by the desire to touch, hold, possess this exquisite being.

The only sounds were the rustle of water and the faint hum of insects. I stood from stacking wood to face her as she stepped from the water, hoping it might be again like that first night we made love, her dazzling nakedness on the back seat of my car, our wild, free lust. Now it seemed she was smiling at me, but maybe I was mistaken. I reached to touch her.

Then there was a thrashing sound in the willows, and someone yelled, "Yo! Anybody around?"

Mol grabbed a towel from the bedroll and clutched it to herself as I called, "Who is it?"

"Just me." It was Kenny emerging from the tall brush. "I went'n dropped my matches in the river and..." He caught sight of Molly, barely covered breast to thigh in wet terrycloth. "Whoa. Sorry. I was, uh, wonderin' if you had any extras. Matches." His thin arms had strange marks on them that I always thought might be needle tracks. But I was never sure.

"Yeah. Here y'go." I had a handful stretched out to him before he took his eyes off Mol.

"Cool. Thanks." He nodded at her, then shot me a goofy leer. I saw he was missing an upper tooth. His Adam's apple bobbed up and down. "See you guys tomorrow." Then he was gone into the willows.

"Shit. Maybe we should be further away," I said.

Molly was silent. Somehow I knew the moment had passed, if it had ever existed at all, but still I tried. I put my hands on her hips, and she turned her back to me. She said, "Don't" with ice in her voice.

"Mmm," I said, and pulled her to me, but she pulled away, and said, "Don't" with not only ice, but a knife-edge of meanness. Suddenly I was boiling with rage; I wanted to just throw her to the ground and force myself on her. But I didn't. I stepped away. I stripped off my clothes and waded into the water.

[IMAGE: 4-07 Camp fire]

Sunset was blazing in the west as I let myself sink neck-deep in the cool, soothing current, and let its insistent pull replace Molly, who was dressing on the bank. Under the water, I masturbated as I dreamed of our bodies together, that union once so simple, now grown so complex, and I let everything go into the river, and afterwards, I felt sad.

Later, under a sky gone indigo, we sat by a fire and made a simple dinner, with no conversation but an occasional "Pass me that cup, please," or "Where's the salt?" We made no eye contact as the sky turned dark and the world seemed to close in, becoming just the circle of dancing light around our fire.

That was when the scorpion came. It was a bizarre little monster with a long jerky shadow, invading our small room. Motionless, we both stared at it as it marched across the sand. Molly's eyes were wide with terror. I very slowly, very carefully picked up a pan from our mess kit, and with a whoop, smashed it down flat on the scorpion. I ground it into the sand, to be sure the thing was dead. But when I picked up the pan, the little beast was gone. Nothing there. Then I got scared. If I couldn't kill it, it could be anywhere, it could spend the night with us, lurking, malevolent, waiting until we sleep, then suddenly wielding that nasty hooked tail to sting us both to painful death.

I went a little wild, stomping the ground, flinging sand with a stick, throwing our supplies all around, yelling, but there was no sign of the scorpion. There was nothing I could do. Molly and I sat in the flicker of the fire and stared at each other, sure that we were doomed.

[IMAGE: 4-29 Night butte silhouette]

Hours passed, our firewood dwindled, and eventually exhaustion took over. We unrolled our sleeping bags under an inky sky spangled with bright stars whose light was blocked only by the black cliffs that loomed across the river. We both slept, and we survived.

As I remember it now, it seems that that was the end of our desert vacation, but in truth it wasn't. For me, the next two days were a blur that I stumbled through, fatigued to my bones as we ate, played, conversed with the others, slept around a big bonfire, then took the long hike and weary drive back to civilization. Molly's injured toe continued to throb, but she stayed off it as much as possible, and with the help of others, me included, got back to the vehicles without incident. Mostly she was quiet those two days, except for the occasional outburst of joking insults toward those she had befriended, that humor that I knew as a cover-up of pain.

We were polite with each other, and considerate. We both pretended, and we did it well, and we went on doing it long after we were home and once again living our normal, everyday lives.

[IMAGE: 5-12 Desert sunset]

A.4 Boulder in a Stream

A.J. WOKE IN DARKNESS, disoriented. He had been dreaming that a woman he didn't recognize had stolen his Nikon and was shooting pictures of him. He was naked and felt embarrassed, but he was also angry that she wouldn't give the camera back. He reached, she moved away. "Just for the bank," she kept saying as she clicked, laughing and taunting him. He had no idea what she meant. Then both his children were there too, all three of them pointing at him and laughing. He realized the woman was his ex-wife although she looked like a stranger. "Ann!" he shouted, and lunged for her throat. But as he shouted, he knew, even in the dream, that Ann was not her name. Then he woke up.

It was 9:57 pm. He ate a bowl of cereal, then dialed his ex-wife's number.

"Mol, it's Jimmy," he said. He didn't like calling himself that, the name of his former self, but he knew that saying "A.J." would only invite ridicule.

Silence for a moment, then a flat "Yes?"

"Remember when we went on that overnight thing in the desert when Lizzie was a baby?"

"Yeah. And?"

"Did you tell anybody about that?"

"Did I tell anybody? Of course. What do you mean?"

"Who?"

"Well, I don't know...my mom, your mom, Carey, Joanne, I don't remember...I mean, it wasn't a secret, it was just a, you know, camping trip. What's the big deal?"

A.J. suddenly wished he had not made this call. He did not like how her voice made him feel small. And he realized it was crazy to be asking her this question. The way Brand had captured his unspoken thoughts was beyond what Molly could have told anyone. There was no betrayal of confidences here. It was something much more strange.

"Nothing. Never mind. Can I talk to Lizzie?"

"Wait. Don't just call and ask weird stuff and then pretend you didn't. What are you trying to get me tangled up in?"

"Nothing. I shouldn't have called. I'm sorry."

"And Lizzie and Max are both asleep, Jimmy. You should know that; it's after ten."

A fragment of a Dylan lyric ran through A.J.'s head and was gone: *And I told you, as you clawed out my eyes, that I never really meant to do you any harm.* He suddenly wanted to curse at her, but he swallowed the urge. "Okay then. Just tell 'em I called. 'Bye."

"Wait, you need to...."

He hung up while she was still speaking.

The divorce, initiated by Molly, had been nasty. She had accused him of adultery—a complete fabrication that was nevertheless a nightmare to counter—and "mental cruelty," a catch-all that apparently applied to husbands who were not at home enough, were always working, were unavailable. He couldn't defend himself against that one; it was true. And it was one of the reasons he had changed his career—without question a good change but still too late to save his marriage.

Now, he hated speaking to her and feeling that old vulnerability seep in like a weakness in his muscles.

A.J. had changed his nickname when he changed his life. His parents and sisters, a few old friends, and Molly, were the only people who still called him Jimmy. He had wanted a new start, a new identity, a new job, a new life. Surely, he had thought, "A.J." would command more respect than "Jimmy" as he ventured from the cubicle of his accounting job into the risky world of freelance photography and video. The passage of time had not shown him to be wrong, and for that he was grateful. Getting by every month was not easy, but he had no regrets.

Fate had been in his favor in one respect: he owed no alimony, and his child support payments were low. His divorce lawyer had been a friendly weakling, no match for the cunning shark his wife had hired, and it appeared to be going very badly during the months of negotiating that led to the final divorce proceedings. But at just the right time, Molly's wealthy uncle had died and left her a huge inheritance. She was set for life, and the kids had trust funds to boot. A.J. was certain she was disappointed that she couldn't punish him further for being an imperfect husband; after all, he knew she would've loved to punish her father for abandoning her mother, and her grandfather for abandoning her grandmother. They had discussed the chain of inherited resentment against the men in her broken family, back in the days when her tears would soak his shoulder and he'd be filled with a huge protective love for her.

Now, despite her lawyer's efforts, she could not convince the court that she needed money. She was awarded only a token payment of two hundred a month for child support. For A.J., newly self-employed, that was a blessed turn of events.

The downside was this: her new affluence and his new poverty meant that custody of the children went entirely to Molly. Not only that, but her attorney gamed the court so well that visitation rights were on her terms alone. To A.J. it was clear: her concern was less about the welfare of the kids than about revenge on him. A preposterous fiction about his daughter's refusal to speak to him was conjured out of thin air, and before he knew what was happening, he was saddled with the humiliation of Supervised Visitation, and only one day a week. He could not bring the kids to his apartment in New York; he had to stay in the New Jersey suburbs, play with them in parks, take them to museums and malls, a skating rink, a zoo, the occasional hike in a bird refuge...all under the analytical gaze of a hired stranger, a social worker from the Supervised Visitation Network.

Every Sunday he complied. To his surprise, much worse than the presence of a chaperone working for his ex was the shocking behavior of his eight-year-old daughter, Elizabeth. She pouted and whined and stubbornly refused nearly everything he suggested, from activities to meals to simply buckling the belt of her car seat. She would throw tantrums like a baby, screaming that she hated him. Her brother Max was his usual (for a six-year-old boy) mellow self, eager to please, but Lizzie's behavior was something entirely new. A.J. never knew whether his sometimes patient, sometimes firm, occasionally angry responses met the unwritten standards of good parenting expected by the ever-present officer of the Custody Police.

First there had been Dorothy, curt and matronly, then Angela, who chatted incessantly and took cigarette breaks, and now it was Pilar, whom he felt sure had suffered abuse and deemed every man guilty. Their exchanges were cordial, but she enforced procedures to the letter.

When a year had passed, A.J. asked Molly to please retract the stipulation of Supervised Visitation. No dice. After another year, he used some of his savings to hire a lawyer to petition the court on his behalf. His appeal was rejected, on the grounds that Lizzie had allegedly told her mother that she was afraid of him. Since then, he'd been saving up for another assault on the court system and researching something called "parental alienation." Even the Supervised Visitation itself was part of Molly's sick compulsion to turn his kids against him, and he wouldn't let her get away with it. The time was almost ripe to try again.

A.J. was pacing the cramped room. *Damn it*, there was already plenty, way too much in fact, occupying his thoughts and his time. And now this—this invisible interloper, stealing the story of his life. *Time to just fucking forget it.*

He considered walking across town to Brownie's in the East Village, where his friend tended bar, and where he might get to see Suzy Diamond. She was a regular there, a painter whose dark-framed face and razor conversation kept a grip on his thoughts the last few weeks. But she had a live-in boyfriend, another painter, who wore lumberjack shirts and paint-splattered work boots. That was a dead end, not a good choice.

He remembered the bagels still in his backpack. He put them in the fridge, grabbed one sesame for his jacket pocket, picked up his tripod and the ever-ready bag full of his 35mm camera gear, and hit the sidewalk, striding with purpose, loving the night streets of New York. The air smelled fresh and the usual bustle on Bleecker seemed uncommonly happy, as if the whole city were welcoming the warming temperatures and clear nights of spring.

At Father Demo Square, he found the perfect view up Sixth Avenue and set up the tripod. He loaded a roll of Ektachrome 160 into his Nikon SLR, attached the quick-release plate using a nickel in the screw slot, and seated the camera on the tripod head with a solid click. He screwed the delicate cable release into the top of the shutter button. Then he framed through his zoom at about 150 mm, with the flow of traffic in the foreground, the Bleecker Street sign at the middle left, and the glowing red and blue spire of the Empire State Building piercing the black sky in the upper right.

These shots were going to be time exposures, turning taxis into streams of light and people into ghosts, all motion gone liquid and translucent, rivers of life flowing through the concrete immoveable canyons of the city. On his budget, film and processing for the sake of experimental art had to be strictly rationed. He had one roll, 36 exposures, to work with tonight, and he hoped for at least one beautiful image. He worked carefully, selecting different combinations of f-stop and shutter speed, writing down each exposure in a tiny notebook. He pushed the plunger of the cable release with his thumb as he counted along with the second hand on his watch, lit by a miniature flashlight held in his teeth. Five seconds, seven seconds, ten seconds, f 5.6, f 8, f 16. For the last third of the roll, he brought out his flash unit and, without attaching it to the camera, held it high over his head and sent a bolt of illumination into the scene as he held the shutter open. Any moving object catching the beam would appear a little more solid than the surrounding swirls of cloudy motion.

He was like a boulder in a stream, standing still while everything flowed around him. With his full attention given to the work, he experienced time in an all-new way. The moment stretched out without limits, nothing existed but the immediate task, all past and future forgotten, his very self and all its stories gone, melted entirely away, merged with the air and sky and all the vibrating waves and particles of the animate and inanimate worlds upon worlds surrounding his centerless center.

It lasted a few minutes, a quarter of an hour, and then he packed up and walked home, smiling.

A.5 Sleuthing

THE NEXT MORNING WAS Saturday. A.J. pulled the hood up on his rain jacket and walked a few blocks through a thin drizzle to the Jefferson Market Library. The building had once been a courthouse with an adjacent women's prison. Its gothic brickwork and multiple arches and soaring clocktower, alternately ominous and beautiful, were a perfect match for the low, dripping sky and the dark mood that brought him here. No reason to delay; the detective work would begin immediately.

His first destination was the stack of fat New York City phone directories, where he found a dozen candidates, R. Brands and Robert Brands, buried in the columns of fine print on the thin yellowing pages. With a shiver of excitement, he wrote them all down in his notebook: names, addresses, phone numbers. He was a sleuth on the trail of a criminal, already closing in! But in the next instant, as he imagined calling each of these strangers, his enthusiasm waned. Maybe he was not cut out for this work. Not only that, but—it suddenly occurred to him—there was no reason to believe the guy was from New York. He could live anywhere, anywhere in the whole world. What next?

A.J. took a deep breath and started again. Detectives use logic. It would be better to conduct the search in the world of writers first; that would narrow the field.

In the hushed light of the tall stained-glass windows, he flicked through the old card catalog. Nothing there. In the basement Reference Room, whose old brick arches and thick walls once held prisoners awaiting trial, he perused several encyclopedias. Again, nothing. With the help of a pretty red-haired librarian, he searched on the computer for any variant of Brand's name. A British baron dead thirty years, a news photographer in Philadelphia, a lawyer who compiled a book of corporate statutes...everything was a dead end.

Hoping that Brand had published in other little magazines like *Espresso Lit*, A.J. began paging through the *Readers' Guide to Periodical Literature*. Bent over a table in the thick underground air of this ghost-ridden room, he scanned volume after slim volume, moving backward in time. The feeling grew that he was in a dungeon; there was a world of light somewhere outside, but he would not see it without a sudden act of desperate will. He straightened his back, took a breath, and decided he had had enough; it was time to surrender. Then, with one more turn of a page, he found what he was looking for. In a nearly-invisible citation for a college literary magazine called *Pratfall*, the Spring 1990 issue, in a list of twenty names under the heading "Fiction and poetry by...," there it was: Robbie Brand.

He almost stood up and shouted. But no, he didn't want a frown from the pretty librarian. In fact, a chance to chat with her would be much better.

Her name was Amanda, but that was as far as he got. She was pleased that he found the writer he was looking for, she told him, but there were no copies of *Pratfall* in this branch. There was a chance he could find it in the Periodicals Room in the main library at 5th and 42nd. Another source would be the Gotham Book Mart on 47th between 5th and 6th. Or he could contact the publisher by mail. She handed him a copy of *Writer's Market* and said, "Good luck."

A.J. looked up *Pratfall* and scribbled their California address in his notebook. The sleuthing business was supposed to be exciting, full of action and drama. It wasn't.

Out on 6th Avenue, the rain had stopped but thick clouds hung over like blankets, muffling the city noise. A.J. stood at the narrow window counter in Gray's Papaya and ate a hot dog with sauerkraut and mustard as he contemplated his next step. There were tasks he needed to do: balance his checkbook, do laundry, call his mom and stepdad, call his kids. He needed to check his answering machine for work messages. He wanted to make some progress on the personal video project he'd started, an art piece inspired by one of his dreams. And he had to get his slides from last night processed. What would be gained by finding Brand's story in *Pratfall*? What if there was no more author information there than had been in *Espresso Lit*? What if the older story had nothing to do with A.J.'s life at all, and *Desert Vacation* was just a fluke? Was he feeling ready to spend more hours in a stuffy library? And what if he searched and searched and found nothing? Did he care anymore?

That's a lot of questions, a voice in his head said. *Who's asking?*

It was the voice of Ashton Gill, the homeless man he'd encountered that night in a Jersey City diner five years ago. "Who's asking?" meant that the most important question at this moment, and at any moment, the question worthy of becoming a permanent state of inquiry, filling every waking hour, the only *real* question, is this one: "Who am I?"

Now *that* was a case for some real detective work, the ultimate sleuthing project.

A.J. decided to listen to this message beamed in from somewhere out there. To once again make that decision, as he'd heard the day before, "...to turn his will and his life over to the care of a power greater than himself...." To let go of this damned tension that had been in his neck all day, and to walk back home on the streets of this city that he loved, and to take pleasure in mindfully handling, one at a time, the details of his actual present life.

B. The Writer

B.1 A Dream

SUN KNIVES CUT MY eyes on every edge of chrome and glass on the cars in this mall lot. Noon, a desert suburb. I sit at the wheel of my dad's old Chrysler, eating greasy fries, chatting with my buddy in the other seat. His name is Mark Twain but he is actually Bob Dylan, 1966, pointy boots and shades. Something is wrong with our high school play and I'm telling him, no, he can't rewrite the script, he just has to play his damned role. A tinny music-box tune comes from behind, but there is only a baby's pink car seat, empty. Far across the baking asphalt, a wall of brown water rises from nowhere, tumbling toward us, fast and slow. Cars crash and roll in a roaring froth, nearer, nearer. There is no key in my ignition. It's all okay. We wait for the wave to arrive.

B.2 Understanding Fiction

THE ASSIGNMENT WAS TO write a story. This seemed impossible, as if he'd been ordered to perform open heart surgery. The boy felt inside himself a vast, if a bit misty, potential; he was sure that someday he'd do something great—but still, this assignment felt like an ambush. The Understanding Fiction class was an elective that he had thought would be a breeze, a no-brainer, occupying time while he decided what his major should be. His father was applying pressure, urging him toward Computer Science. "Try and be practical for once!" never stopped echoing in his ears.

Computer Science...all those ones and zeros. He didn't know what he wanted, but he knew it wasn't that.

The young man's name, to his own dismay, was Brandt Robaczynski. He was forever spelling it, first and last, slowly, for institutional drones. His dad assured him it was a respectable name, held by respectable men before him. But those men were dead, or worse yet, European, so he wasn't convinced.

Among his friends, Brandt was respected for two things: first, for his encyclopedic knowledge of James Bond—the *real* Bond, the one in the Ian Fleming novels, not the movies (not even the Sean Connery ones; he was a dedicated purist). And, a fading second, for the impressive, even inspired, moves he'd occasionally displayed during his two seasons playing goalie on the otherwise pathetic Newton High School soccer team.

Brandt's English 213 professor at William Paterson College was Philip Covello, who held the belief that nothing could help a bunch of college sophomores understand the great writers better than doing some writing of their own. Covello observed the short story form wilting in the garden of American letters, and he felt this to be a great tragedy, especially since he'd been slaving a decade on his own collection, for which he was now in search of a publisher. His directive to Brandt's class was to write a story using the tools of fiction—in other words, "...make it about someone other than yourself, or if you can't do that, then just disguise yourself somehow. Please."

The assignment had been given at the beginning of the semester, with the story not due until a week before finals; there was no excuse for not getting it done. But with only nine days left till the deadline, Brandt had written nothing. He imagined the shame of failing the class: his friends' hoots, his professor's silent condescension, his father's dark scowl. He was filled with rage at the injustice of the world, but he still couldn't write a single sentence. And then, on May 7, 1989, his fortune changed.

He was working his regular Saturday morning shift at the desk of the Marina Vista Motel in Lake Hopatcong when one of the maids, Lourdes, brought in a yellow legal pad covered from first page to last with handwriting. She had found it under the bed in room 11 and thought the previous night's tenant should be notified. Brandt looked up the registration information; it showed an address in Sparta, just a few miles up Route 15, but there was no phone number. To ease his habitual boredom at the desk, he began to read the scrawls on the yellow pages.

The handwriting was sometimes difficult to decipher, as if the writer were drunk or in a hurry, as if the sentences were not really meant to be read. But as he worked his way through, it began to form an articulate story told in a clear voice. He wasn't more than three pages in and feeling a growing fascination with the scene unreeling before him, when a delicious, frightening idea sprang to the surface of his mind. He had to put the pad down on the counter and take a slow breath to face the thought: this scribbled story by a person he'd never met could become *his* story. No one would ever know. Maybe he didn't have to fail Understanding Fiction after all.

With a whole new enthusiasm, he continued reading. He told himself that he hadn't decided yet what he would do; that such a leap outside the bounds of ethics would take some serious consideration. It was years later before he was able to admit that, in some deeper place within himself, he had known immediately that the future was set. As if, at the very moment the notepad appeared, the events had begun to unfurl inevitably, and all he could do was ride the racing wave like a stick of driftwood, helpless, toward some invisible shore.

As he read, the spiky squiggles of black ink etched in stark relief on the yellow paper seemed to flow and jump like music. They overpowered the weak blue rules that traversed the pages, searing jerky patterns into Brandt's retinas; their graphic rhythms would plague his dreams for years to come. He leaned back in his chair, ignoring the sunshine that streamed into the empty office and, page after page, peered into the private darkness of a total stranger. The pages were apparently written by a man named Angus James Campbell, whose marriage was coming to an end; that's why he'd spent the night in a motel when he lived nearby. The tale Campbell told revealed his domestic life and some of his past, but Brandt's impression was that those were mostly just a side-plot. The setting of the story was a roadside diner on the previous evening, where Campbell had met a mysterious traveler and witnessed some inexplicable events. He had apparently written this narrative in the wee hours of the morning, this very morning, after pacing his motel room all night. Brandt didn't know what to believe: was this account "true" in a literal sense, was it some sort of hallucination that Campbell accepted as fact, or was the whole thing just an exercise in creative writing—a big lie?

When he finished the last page and put the notepad down, Brandt's feelings were mixed. The narrator of the story had touched something in him; he felt a whisper of kinship, even brotherhood, with this man he'd never met. At the same time, the thrill of voyeurism was blooming in him like a stain, made more complex by the knowledge that he had not only peeked into someone's private life, but that he was considering exploiting that life for his own benefit. Or, if the story was a fabrication, he was considering stealing another person's creative work, which was equally heinous. His palms were sweaty and his breath short. He felt simultaneously solemn, excited, and guilty.

As the vibrations of the story's dark atmosphere began to dissipate into the sunny air of this typical Saturday morning, Brandt began to analyze his options. First, he asked himself, what were the risks of such an act of plagiarism? Of course, if he were caught, he would fail English 213, and possibly face additional disciplinary action by the college. But he was a good student, and well-behaved; he doubted such a minor infraction would permanently derail his schooling or career, such as it was. And anyway, how would he get caught? Chances seemed extremely slim that a family man who worked in New York City and lived in Sparta would have any contact with a professor at William Paterson, thirty miles away in Wayne. And even if Campbell were to discover the theft, what could he do? After all, this was not a published work whose value in the marketplace had been established. It was just some personal scribblings by a nobody, borrowed by another nobody for a class assignment at an unimportant school, to be read by one professor only. Where's the crime?

The key was to avoid the humiliation of exposure. One way was to rewrite the story so substantially that he could plausibly deny any plagiarism. But to Brandt that seemed as impossible as writing a story from scratch. And besides, he didn't have time. So, he deduced, the smartest action was to cover his tracks in whatever way he could, and go forward with the plan. Which, he realized with that thought, had now moved out of the realm of the hypothetical. He could no longer fool himself that he was merely pondering plagiarism as an academic question of ethics. It was now a plan.

First, Brandt slid the legal pad carefully into his backpack. Next, he pulled a county phone directory out of the desk and paged through until he found a listing for A.J. Campbell, with an address that matched the motel register. And there was a phone number. Brandt immediately slammed the book shut before the number could imprint itself on his consciousness. He had already resolved not to trace the notepad's owner, and to pretend that the pad had been thrown in the trash by the housekeepers if Campbell came back looking for it. But...he found it more than interesting that the directory listing suggested the tale was not fiction; Campbell had used his real name in the story, so maybe the rest of it was also true. Unless, of course, last night's lodger was not Campbell at all. Or the story was written by someone else entirely. The possibilities were endless, and endlessly distracting. Brandt shrugged them off and continued his mission.

His next move was to walk the length of the motel until he saw Lourdes pushing her housekeeping cart out of a room. He pretended it was an accidental encounter and, oh, by the way, he had called the notepad's rightful owner, who asked him to throw the pad in the trash, that it was worthless. So, he told Lourdes, that's what he did.

That evening, he called his friend Kumar to cancel their plan for hanging out together. Brandt decided to tell something like the truth. "I really gotta work on my English paper," he said.

"Oh, so now you're gonna start on that thing? I thought you were going for an F, man."

"Well, I finally got some ideas, so I gotta start writing."

Kumar was skeptical. "Really? What ideas?"

"I'll tell you later. Or let you read it. Maybe. Tell me how the game goes."

He gave the same speech to his father as they shared takeout Chinese for dinner. His backpack, burning with its secret, hung on the back of Brandt's chair.

"Okay, good. Get 'er done," his dad said through a mouthful of lo mein. "I'm picking up Miriam at work and we're going out, catch some music or something. I may stay over there tonight."

Brandt was glad to have the evening alone, although the silent house had never lost the weird air of breathless expectation it had acquired six years ago when his mother never returned from the hospital.

As the sound of his father's truck faded down the street, he pulled out the notepad, set it in the light of his desk lamp, then laid next to it a new spiral notebook open to the first page. It seemed to him that the smart approach was to do everything possible to surround his purloined tale with the aura of authenticity, so his plan was to transcribe the entire thing by hand into his own notebook, then destroy Campbell's legal pad. So, there it would be; an original draft in his own handwriting, indisputable. He sat, adjusted his chair, picked up his favorite rolling-ball fine-point pen, and began writing. In an unexplored part of himself, there was more to this task than the careful calculations of a forger. Something akin to superstition, mixed with a guilty sort of respect, guided his fingers to copy Campbell's sentences and paragraphs exactly as they were written—punctuation errors, sentence fragments, everything—even cross-outs and margin notes. He felt such mirroring to be required somehow, as if he owed it to Campbell... but also because something, some instinct he could not have verbalized, told him that the only way to make this story his own was to live the process of writing it, to set each word upon the page as if he were truly the author. To inhabit by imitation. Like an actor, to take the playwright's words into his body and send them back out again as his own spontaneous creation.

As he wrote, the task pulled him into itself, as if into a cave, deeper and deeper, further from daylight. The house and everything else outside his little circle of lamplight receded into darkness and disappeared. The scenes he was writing played themselves out in front of his inner eye, a private movie. He imagined hearing a voice, not his own, speaking the words as he wrote them. The pain of the narrator's cry to his wife was palpable, a lump in Brandt's own chest, and when, in the story, lightning crackled and the diner's lights went out, he flinched in his chair. Brandt had no idea how much time had passed when, on a page blurred by an inexplicable film of tears, he carefully inscribed the final words: ...*across the sky.*

Brandt put the pen down, sat back, and took a deep breath. He flexed his right fingers, cramped from writing. The house was quiet. He heard a passing car several streets away, then nothing more. He knew what he had to do, although it pained him to think of it. He put a stop to all thought, grabbed the yellow legal pad, marched to the back door, and stepped outside into the chilly night. On the deck in crisp, pine-scented moonlight, he lifted the lid of the barbecue grill, found the lighter in its usual place, and struck a flame. Shivering in his t-shirt, he held the notepad up by its spine, touched the tiny fire to its pages until the flame began to climb, then dropped the sudden conflagration onto the wire grate and watched the mass of scribbled leaves blaze up, blacken, curl, flutter, turn to smoke, and disappear. For a moment, he felt bathed in flickering light and feeble warmth, but then was plunged again into darkness and cold as he stared, not moving. He took the bitter haze of burnt paper and ink deep into his lungs and breathed it out, a cloud now mixed with his own essence. Finally, he raised his eyes to watch a few tiny orange sparks lift toward the stars and wink out, as a whisper of breeze stirred the last charred flakes and sent the final wisp of smoke into airy oblivion.

To say that Brandt was surprised by the events of the following weeks would be an understatement. First, as he did his struggling best to clean up the story's most egregious violations of the rules of English composition, then typed it painstakingly on a computer in the college library, he observed himself not only feeling a growing possessiveness of its every word, phrase, and sentence, but also experiencing a foreign, delicious pleasure with every reading of the text—his text. Then, he handed the story in to Mr. Covello—on the deadline, and with a clear conscience…mostly. There was not a trace of the fear he'd begun with, that his crime would be discovered. But still, occasionally, a sensation of himself as a slinking, guilty creature would rise up unexpectedly and he would be, for a moment, fully aware that somewhere not many miles away were a man and wife whose private lives Brandt had violated. Then, within seconds, that awareness would sink back into the murky current of everyday life, disappearing as if it had never existed.

He let himself forget about it entirely during finals week—all that cramming, coffee, concentration. In the semester's last English 213 class, after the tumult of tests was over, he was stunned when Covello stood at the front of the room, waved Brandt's manuscript in the air, and said with entirely unexpected enthusiasm, "This! This is what we want!"

As Brandt sat blushing, Covello paced back and forth in front of the class, gesturing with the sheaf of papers clutched in his right hand, speaking as if to himself, but loudly.

"In this story, unpretentiously titled 'The Tunnel Diner,' we see what a young author can do when he combines a bold imagination, writerly craft, and an instinct for the potentials of postmodern literature. What Brandt has done here is inhabit the mind of someone rather different from himself and, without resorting to stock situations or characters from TV or movies, create a heartfelt cry in the night. The first-person narrator that Brandt has created is an ordinary man, a man whose life is unraveling—his job is torture, and worst of all, he's losing his marriage and family. That's what the story is really about, but just like in real life—in our mental lives at least—there's a great deal of other stuff intruding, to distract, to confuse. Human psychology is complex and sensitive. Is the narrator going crazy? What is reality? The story gives us questions, not answers, and uses a meta-fictional device that is both postmodern and as old as Scheherazade: the text within a text—the story that includes another story, which includes yet another story. Bits of arcane knowledge are introduced to build an undercurrent of mystery...."

Covello went on and on, stopping occasionally to read passages from Brandt's typewritten pages. To Brandt's ears, the phrases he had thought he owned now sounded foreign, and the things Covello was saying about the story were not at all what Brandt had thought interesting or important. In fact, half of what the professor was saying was entirely beyond Brandt's understanding. He had worried that his fraud would be utterly transparent: after all, how could he, a shallow nineteen-year-old from rural New Jersey, possibly have come up with all that weird stuff...marital relations, Utah and Mormons, even Native American folktales, of all things?

Covello spoke without sarcasm and Brandt stared at his desktop in confusion, steeped in a mixture of shame and pleasure. He felt the eyes of the other students on him, but he couldn't look up. When the ordeal was over, he composed his face into a mask that he hoped would convey humble confidence, with an appreciative little smile, as Covello said to him, "Brandt, let's talk for a few minutes after class."

COVELLO HAD HIGHER AIMS for the story. A literary journal for undergraduate writers was holding a fiction contest whose deadline was near. Besides genuinely believing that "The Tunnel Diner" had a chance at winning, Covello knew that it would look good for him in the eyes of the college administration to have a literary winner emerge from one of his classes. He felt almost paternal about wanting to guide Brandt toward what may be his life's calling.

(A few years later, when Professor Covello read "The Tunnel Diner" again in the published collection that bore its name, he wondered why he had been so enthusiastic about it. This time it seemed rather more pedestrian. Can't a good work stay good? Is all virtue ephemeral? Once again, he fell into his old pattern of doubting his judgment, his teaching ability, even his own writing talent. For several long minutes, he suffered. But with another ten seconds of sober reflection, he remembered the context. That had been a year when he felt continually dismayed by the inarticulate blunders of college sophomore bulls thrashing about in the china closet of literature. By comparison to everyone else in his class, Brandt had been surprisingly brilliant. And after all, the story did go on to win an award and get published, so Covello's opinion, rendered in the slant of the moment, had been seconded. One more writer's career was launched, he mused. Is that good? Well, how can we judge? It all fades into the past, anyway, doesn't it?)

ON THAT LAST DAY of the semester, as Covello told Brandt about how to enter the literary journal's contest, his tone held not a trace of the faint condescension Brandt thought he had always heard in it before. To Brandt, it seemed distinctly possible that he was being treated as an equal, a professional colleague. Wearing his mask to cover the daze he felt, he listened to his professor's instructions, wrote down the contest information, and left the classroom. Yes! To win an award of some kind, any kind—that would be great! Not likely, of course, but still...worth a gamble. Even to be able to claim creatorship of something public, something in print. He could be somebody. With single-minded focus, he walked directly to the library computer room, made a few minor edits that Covello had marked in red on the pages, and printed out the new final version of the story.

However, it turned out that he had to print the story twice, because as he leafed through the pages fresh off the printer, the name "Angus James Campbell" jumped out like a fist slamming his chest. Suddenly short of breath, he returned to the keyboard and meticulously changed the names, everywhere they appeared in the story, of the real author and his wife. Their children too. Searching the document, he scolded himself silently, appalled at his blundering oversight. Apparently, he'd grown so convinced that the story was his own invention, that he could have let the single most incriminating bit of evidence to the contrary slip out into public view. The real author's identity! How could he have been so stupid? And the fact that Mr. Covello and the students in his class had glimpsed the truth...well, what could be done now? He had no choice: he had to let go of that nasty niggle of worry and just put all his faith in the blessed odds.

It took Brandt no more than a minute to invent new names: Angus James Campbell, also called Jimmy, became Jefferson Carter, or Jeff (it had a truthful ring, he thought). Molly, sometimes Mol, became just Ann (his first girlfriend's middle name). The children got the generic Laura and Ricky. Simple. The other characters' names he left as they were—surely they were inconsequential, if not entirely fictional already.

He felt a great relief as he watched on the screen, one by one, the fictional names, his own creations, obliterating the real-life names. As if he were killing the actual human beings these strings of letters stood for, the Campbell family—erasing them from his life and his conscience, once and for all.

He checked for other clues. The name of Campbell's employer, he replaced with "major chemical company." A couple of towns and a river he'd never heard of...no problem, they would stay. Jersey City and the Tunnel Diner...nothing incriminating there, so he left them alone. One final stroke: the "Marina Vista Motel" became the "Bridgeview." Done.

He returned to the title page and was just about to give the Print command when one more thing caught his attention: his own name, sitting there under the story's title like a lame joke, an implausible jumble of consonants and vowels. It had to go. He remembered a name he had once fantasized for himself, back in his early teens when he was trying on for size various Bond-like personas. Under the title, backspacing letter by letter, he deleted "Brandt Robaczynski." Then, in its place, he typed "Robbie Brand." Much, much better. Infinitely better. The thrill he felt was visceral, a momentary ripple in the tissues; he wasn't even aware that with that last keystroke, he had finally crossed the threshold toward which he'd been inexorably moving these last few weeks. With neither mourning nor celebration, the thing was done: the death of his past self, the birth of an all-new self. A new self that would lead the former Brandt Robaczynski down paths he could never have imagined.

For him, now, it seemed more important that he had changed the names of the identifiable characters in the story, but he did intend the courtesy of telling his professor he was entering the contest under a pseudonym. After the document was saved on a diskette and the printed manuscript, along with a polite cover letter, was safely in the mail, he destroyed every typed copy of earlier drafts. He even went back to his handwritten first draft, thoroughly scribbled out the original names, and wrote in the new ones. Now there was no trace left of the people whose lives he had stolen. Jimmy and Molly were dead and buried. He was finally free of them.

Or so he thought. His mind, that unruly animal, would not let them go. Their tenancy in his head was far from over; in fact, it had barely begun.

B.3 "The Tunnel Diner," a Short Story by Robbie Brand

I CAN'T SLEEP, ALTHOUGH it's dawn. I know it's dawn by the gray light leaking in around the edges of the blackout curtain in this drab motel room. How fitting. There have been times when it seemed like I was always in this darkness, like I might see a dim light around the edges of my life, but the window that would show me why things are as they are in this world was forever blacked out.

I was just thinking that maybe if I write down what has happened tonight, or rather last night, then maybe I can make some sense of it.

Mostly, it happened in a diner at the mouth of the Holland Tunnel, Jersey side. The Tunnel Diner, "Open 24 Hours Since 1942," is nothing special. I mean, besides some stainless steel accents, it has very little "classic diner" charm. In fact, it is utterly devoid of anything resembling charm, except that it's the place where I met Ashton Gill. Maybe that's where this story begins.

But no story, especially one taking place in a roadside diner, really has a beginning. The Big Story goes on and on, without beginning or end, like the endless spaghetti network of interstates and two-lanes that tangle and weave their way across this country. Or maybe like a woven rug of infinitely multicolored strands ripped from the rags of eons of grandmothers, a rag rug that covers the cosmos like a linoleum kitchen floor. The Tunnel Diner has a tattered, faded piece of rag rug in its doorway, so I guess that's how *this* story ties into the Big Story. At least, that's the way Ashton might have said it, I imagine.

Ashton Gill was a hitchhiker. He said his occupation was "excursionist." Actually, what he said was "excursionist and eavesdropper on the whispers of the universe," but all that was a little too much for me to take in just then—the ramblings of a homeless eccentric. Ashton had never been to the East Coast before, so naturally his destination was New York City. He'd have been there easily if it weren't for the ceaseless bickering of the two college girls who'd picked him up in Allentown, Pennsylvania on their way to a club-hopping weekend in Manhattan. They had stopped for him because they thought maybe he was holding some coke. When he said with a smile, *no, I maintain a natural high*, they became decidedly less friendly. An hour later, their shrill arguments over fingernail polish and boyfriends had rubbed a raw sore on his serenity, as he put it. The highway wasn't so high anymore. So, as they neared New York and he gazed enchanted at the skyline of the holy city, he could stand for no more petty sacrilege. *Will you two shut the fuck up!* he had exploded from the back seat as they pulled away from the Turnpike toll booth.

Swerve, screech, door pop, door slam, engine roar.

They never got a chance to see that he was always so quick to smile again after these little explosions; it was just his way, it didn't mean anything.

So Ashton found himself walking the mile-long ramp to the tunnel along the white line between a three-foot concrete barrier and lanes of roaring trucks. The barrier kept him from falling a hundred feet into the darkness that was Jersey City. And there It was: Oz, Camelot, ancient Thebes, the Seven Cities of Cibola. Across rooftops, across water, but seeming so close he could reach out his hand and pluck tiny emeralds from its windows...that glittering fantastic stack of gold and jewels that even now at midnight looked alive and screaming: Manhattan. Destiny!

And Ashton was glad he was walking. *The better to hear the songs of his fate*, he said. Suddenly he loved the choking exhaust of trucks, loved the dangerous whoosh as speeding drivers clipped past him from behind, loved the nip of the March air. He whistled, then sang, then whooped and howled, and knew that no one could hear him above the highway rumble, but his silent shouts carried across the air to meet the silent din of the city and mingle into a crazy love song over the Hudson. All this is how he told it to me later, in the Tunnel Diner.

But I'm way ahead of myself. This mental racing is a problem I have. I get distracted from the business at hand; maybe it's one of the reasons I'm sitting here in the Bridgeview Motel instead of sleeping next to my wife in my own bed, at home, just a few miles away. Or maybe that's because of other things, things beyond my control, plans made in other spheres, I really don't have the faintest idea.

I was heading home from another late night at the office and as often happened, I'd started feeling sleepy in the middle of the tunnel, with another forty-five minutes of driving ahead of me. I stopped at the diner for coffee-to-go and collided with Ashton in the doorway. I must have been a little blind, because I was full of hatred. Angry. Fed up. Bitter.

I was carved out of stone; I was cast in cement. If someone ever made a statue of Dr. Jekyll's Mr. Hyde, I could have been the model for it last night. A granite hunchback with a scowl and hands poised for violence, that's what I felt like. Anger turned inward becomes depression, I've heard. So I was depressed. Angry, depressed, hateful, bitter—whatever. But with a smile frozen on my face most of the time.

It's because of my goddamned job. Over and over in my head, I bitch and moan, *what could be less fucking important in the fucking universe than these fucking fiscal-year-end reports?* But day after day, in a windowless cubicle, I'm expected to feel as though this is life and death; nothing else matters. And I'm trapped. A mortgage, two cars, two kids, a wife.

A wife. It was after eleven. I was expected home two hours earlier, and I hadn't called. I've given up calling because she thinks it's a lie anyway. She believes I'm cheating on her whenever I work late. Welcome to another night of hell.

So anyway, I stopped at the diner for coffee. The air had that feel of a storm approaching, no stars, a deeper darkness boiling in from the west. As I entered, the neon sign above my head that said DINER spelled downwards like a crossword, buzzed, flickered, went all the way off. Usually just the N or R was weak or gone, but now the whole sign went black. Just for a moment, then it blazed on again, with a crackle and the smell of ozone. I got my coffee and as I was heading out the door, Ashton entered, swinging off his backpack. It hit my cup, spilling coffee all over the rag rug. Suddenly it was like lightning flashed in the cloud over my head. I looked up at him with hatred, ready to kill.

His smile was wide open. "Oh, man, I'm sorry. Lemme buy you another one, huh?"

The concrete set of my jaw wouldn't let me speak or return the smile, but he just kept talking. To the waitress: "Another coffee for the man in the suit here, please. And sorry about the spill." To me: "Bad day, huh? Or just a long day? Maybe a long, bad day. I've had a few myself, I know how you're feelin,' man. Hey, take a break. Let's get that coffee in a real cup and sit down here and relax a little before hitting the mean old highway. Whadya say?"

Normally I would have said no thanks. But there was something in his speech, a faint western twang, a little too much tongue in the R's, that sounded like my own. The crinkled eyes, the sun- and wind-burned skin that added age to a face not much older than mine, reminded me of the honest, hard-working farmers of my childhood, even though his hair hung in tangles to his shoulders, his chin showed several days' growth of stubble, and his faded jeans were not clean. And it was odd that under his denim jacket were a crisp white collarless shirt and a vest of rich black and red brocade. I'm not sure why, but I followed him to a booth away from the door. We were the only customers in the place.

He tasted the coffee. "Mmm, just what I needed."

"Where you from?" I asked. I seemed to be getting some flexibility back in my facial muscles.

"Who's askin'?" He grinned.

"Sorry. Jefferson Carter. Jeff."

"Ashton Gill." We shook hands. A little of the steel inside me melted. "Vernal, Utah," he said.

"No shit? I'm from Richfield." I expected a surprised reaction from him, but his eyes only crinkled a little deeper as he smiled and nodded slowly.

I shook my head, feeling drawn to get a reaction from him. "Not many Utah boys in the jungles of Jersey. Strange coincidence, huh?"

"Well, I don't really believe in coincidence, but 'strange' is a pretty accurate word."

It was strange all right, how I was starting to feel okay with this guy. I mean he looked like, at best, some aging Deadhead hitchhiker. At worst, a career criminal. So maybe it was just the fact that, despite my ugly mood, I liked his face. But that's one of my problems. I like a lot of faces. I stare. The lines and planes, the wrinkles and curves, the glimpse of something eternal in the eyes—it's like an addiction, a visual addiction I can't break. I just love people's faces. That's why I'm a photographer.

Actually, I'm an accountant for a major chemical company. That's what I *am*. In my dreams I'm a photographer. Only in my dreams.

This thing with faces has been no end of problems. My wife hates it. Of course, she only sees me stare at the women—the young, beautiful women. She doesn't believe that I stare just as much at the old, wrinkled women, at the young men, at the people of middle age, at children, at anyone whose face says something to me about beauty, the beauty of the vast cosmos and its expression in the individual human, etc. etc. In my mind I compose the frame,

I light the face; I've taken a million beautiful portraits without a camera, without film, with eyes only.

My camera sits under some old shoes at the bottom of a closet. There was a time when in a spasm of passion I told my beautiful young wife that I was all hers forever, that for her I'd give up anything. *I'll take this bag of camera equipment and pitch it in the river today if you want me to.* I meant it. Of course, she never asked me to do such a thing. She didn't have to ask. Her feelings toward my "little hobby" were clear. If ever the camera was pointed in her direction, she would duck, turn away, protest in anger. Once, with much cajoling, I got her to model nude for me but when she saw the beautiful images, her reaction was disgust. I took to spending weekends roaming the hillsides alone with my camera, rather than at home. Then when I asked a girlfriend of hers to model for me, no nudity, just portraits, things got ugly.

And I believed in honoring my promises. It was a silent agreement that happened over time. My camera went "in the river" under the shoes and for years she thought it was because I lost interest and grew to love accountancy. We're light years apart.

"Menus?" the waitress asked. As she spoke, a feeble smile passed across the bottom half of her face and was gone. She reminded me of a double-scoop ice cream cone. Big and round on top, in a voluminous white shirt, tails out, and black stretch pants that tapered down over skinny legs. Over one breast was embroidered in script, "Felicity." Her hair was the color of butterscotch but dark at the roots. Her face was round, pale, pretty, but her eyes were tired.

"Just coffee for me," I said.

"I'll have a bacon cheeseburger and fries, with the bacon not too crisp if you don't mind, Felicity." Ashton smiled up at her. "Nice name. Means happiness." Her lips curled briefly. She seemed to be looking somewhere else, inside maybe.

"Mm-hm. I'll see if Achmed can handle that," she said as she turned away. *Achmed*—the way she said it sounded like spitting.

The swarthy bald man behind the counter called out in our direction, "Miss America taking good care of you guys over there?" He spoke English thickly, as though with a mouthful of glue.

"Fine, thanks," I said. When I looked back at Ashton, he was staring at Achmed. Just a beat, then he looked back at me with a smile.

"So, Jeff, you came to New York for what reason?"

"Work. Money. Career."

"So you came here to be the world's greatest accountant?"

I snorted. "Right. And how did you know I'm an accountant?"

"Just a hunch." He pulled a napkin from the holder. "Seriously, is that why you came here, to the center of the world? You upset the grace of living when you lie, as Tim Hardin said."

I wasn't about to tell this stranger about my dreams and problems. When the opportunity to transfer to New York came up three years ago, I took it for two reasons: one that I told Ann—career advancement—and one that I kept to myself. I had dreamed of making it in the world of photography. I thought that if I could be near New York, I could pull my camera out of the closet (after all, it had been in there five years), work nights and weekends on a portfolio, and start peddling my work to agents, stock houses, publishers, all those places that New York has so many of.

I started by opening a business checking account in my name only. Ann blew up. I told her it was a smart thing to do, a tax write-off. We could deduct all my photo expenses, even vacations and shots of the kids. We could save money. She didn't buy this for a second. She knew I'd been hiding secret plans from her. She accused me of wanting to steal money from her, of plotting to get rid of her, run away with somebody, cheat her out of all that was hers. That was the first time she brought up "the woman from Denver."

Oh, man. I'm struggling to get to the root of it all.

Ann, Ann, what happened to us? So much time has passed, I don't know how to talk about this.

Part of the dark cloud of my anger when I stopped at the diner was because I was expected at home by nine and it was already after eleven, and I was tired of this goddamned "reporting in" that she expects. Another fifteen-hour day in the office, and at the end of all that, why should I have to worry about proving I'm faithful to a woman who'll never believe it anyway?

It's now early Wednesday morning. On Monday night, when I got home about eleven, she said, "I won't be made a fool of any longer. I've spoken to a twenty-four-hour locksmith. It wouldn't be hard to get these locks changed at a moment's notice. And I could get a restraining order to keep you away from the kids."

Threats, always the bullshit threats, so exhausting. "What are you talking about?" I said.

"That woman from Denver called again," she said.

The problem is, I do not now nor have I ever known a woman from Denver. Three years ago I went there on a business trip, two nights alone in a hotel, a day of boring meetings, two long plane flights, no woman, no nothing. I'm innocent, so I'm faced with these choices: one, someone's playing a practical joke on me; two, my wife is lying for some reason that I can't comprehend, except that it feels malicious; and three, she's seriously disturbed, in the grip of a hallucination. I wish I could say I was certain it wasn't number two or three, but I've lived with her for eight years now. I'm sad to see her like this. I don't know what to do.

And I'm worried about the damage being done to our kids by all the bickering, the shouts and insults. Laura, at six, is pretty savvy; there's no more pretending everything's okay. Ricky is only four and seems oblivious to everything but his action figures, but I suspect he understands more than he lets on. Still, despite the tender little ears listening, Ann and I just can't get through a day without conflict. I feel terrible for our babies.

It wasn't always this way between us. Once we were in love. Now I'm remembering things I haven't thought of in so long. For a few months just before and after we were married, we rented a trailer several miles out of town, surrounded by pastures, on the edge of a bluff overlooking the Sevier River. We had two puppies, a chubby Husky mix and a hyperactive little black Lab. Weekends, they chased Ann around the fields as she tagged along with me. All my attention was absorbed in photographing the delicate wildflowers in the dawn, or the golden slant of sunset on the rocks along the river. Sometimes she grew silent, and I liked it that way.

Our bed was a mattress on the floor. I had just started with the company, the same company I'm with now, but then I was a warehouse laborer as I worked on my accountancy certification. She had a fast-food job. Some days, many days, we both called in sick, unable to part our sweaty flesh. Even her newfound pregnancy couldn't calm our lust. We giggled, breathless, as we took turns with the phone, still tangled in the sheets, me still inside her, growing hard again, and after making excuses to our bosses, falling deeply once more into the dark tangle of lips and tongues, the slow, exquisite slither of skin on wet skin. Afterwards, one of us would get up and let the dogs in.

That goofy pair, all paws and tails and tongues, would come bounding and tumbling down the hall to attack us with licks, rolling and jumping in the sheets, yelping with puppy joy. Our life was good. So, sure, we had a fight now and then. But we were happy.

Those weeks were the beginning of the end of our Mormonism, the religion I'd been brought up wholeheartedly believing, and she had joined soon after we met. The divine miracle of sex had suddenly shown to me a new God, a God nothing like the puritanical old white man who had hovered over the heads of everyone I knew for so long. Together, in the grip of Eros, Ann and I unfurled to new ways of thought, more open, more free, less guilty...and I've always been grateful for her company on that journey, the journey that has led me to the here and now. But it wasn't my way to blurt all this to strangers.

Ashton had asked me why I came to New York, but I countered his question with one of my own. "What about you? How did you end up here?"

He laughed. "I'd hardly call this the end. I just got here. Haven't even been into the Big Apple yet."

"What I meant was why."

"When John Lennon was asked the same question, he said that if he'd been around in the glory days of the Roman Empire, he'd have lived in Rome, because it was the capital of the world. Today that's New York. Same for me. It's the center, and I've been walking the outer edges all this time. The outer edges are a necessary place to go, but so is the center, right? Axis Mundi."

"Okay. So...do you have a job or something?"

"Oh, I have a job alright. I just never know what it is until I find it. Around here I guess they'd give me the official title of Homeless

Man." And he went on to tell me the story of his arrival here, and to give me his own job description: excursionist, eavesdropper, etc. etc. As he spoke, I began to be aware that the coffee I'd been drinking didn't seem to be working. I felt warm and drowsy, my flesh melting into the blue leatherette seat.

"Come closer," Ashton said. "I want to tell you something. There's a great darkness out there, greater than you know. And it's full of sound. Look...."

He pulled the hair back from over his right ear. Sleepy as I was, I flinched. It was red and swollen, half again as big as an ear should be. "I can hear very well with this ear, despite its appearance. It's really nothing. Let me tell you the story."

I shrugged; I was in his hands. He went on, "I was a kid, maybe nine. It was dead winter and a blizzard outside. I had one of those coats with a zip-off hood, and I had left the hood over at my cousin's, where I'd spent the weekend. My mother told me to wear my sister's stocking hat, with the pompom on top. Ha. No way I was showing up like that. So I walked a mile to school with nothing covering my ears, wind chill probably 20 below, hitting my right side. By the time I got to class, my ear looked like this. It burned like crazy for the whole day, then went numb. But that night my mom, well, first she cried a little, but then she put her warm hands on it and prayed for like an hour. Really. I fell asleep. Anyway, it's had this lovely appearance ever since. But guess what? I can hear things you can't."

Inside, I was still. Inside, I jumped with disbelief. I was skeptical. I was pretending to be skeptical. Which was it? I don't know. I said, "Uh-huh. Right. Like a dog."

"Better. For instance, right now, in the kitchen, the cook is telling the waitress that she might as well face it, he's going to fuck her sooner or later and she's gonna love it. She hates him."

"Bullshit. You can't hear that." My blood roused a little from the growing stupor, but I felt my protestation to be only half-hearted. A moment later, Felicity came out of the kitchen looking a little pale and began clearing a table with motions that seemed much too violent. She dropped a cup and it shattered. She bit her lip and held back tears.

Ashton beckoned me closer to him, and I obeyed, without a will of my own. He leaned across the table until our noses almost met. His voice was a smooth, perfectly audible whisper. "Now look at this one."

He pulled the hair back from his left ear. This time I groaned and looked away. It wasn't an ear at all. Just a tangled mass of scar tissue surrounding a hole in his head.

"This one has a more interesting story. I was about twenty, a wild kid. I hung around with two brothers, Paiute Indians. We raised hell. We drank a lot. We ate peyote and datura. We cruised the hills and shot prairie dogs randomly, from the road. Those little gophers would stand up on the rims of their holes and sniff the air, and I would point my .22 rifle out the window of the pickup and blow them away. Thought it was fun, at the time. Anyway, my Paiute buddies, Norbert and Ray, had a pet badger—one of the wildest of wild creatures, the gophers' tough-guy cousin, the warrior. One day I was totally gone in a peyote trance when the Lord of the Animals appeared, standing above me in the sun. First, he spoke to me of sacrifice—of how you must give up the things you feel are precious, for that is the only way to grow from being a child to being a man. Then he told me about Badger. He said it like this...."

Ashton's voice seemed to take on a different character, distant, faintly foreign.

"Long ago, Badger always carried darkness in a sack on his back. One day he was traveling along when he met Coyote. Coyote was certain there was something delicious in the bag, so he said, 'My cross-cousin, you look tired. Let me carry your heavy load.' But Badger refused. Coyote asked over and over again, until Badger finally let him carry the sack. Of course, Coyote immediately snuck behind a bush and opened the sack. When everything suddenly began to get dark, he grew scared and called to Badger, 'Help, help, my cross-cousin! Something terrible was in your pack! I can hardly see!' Badger immediately spread his arms wide and gathered the darkness back in. 'You should not have opened my pack,' Badger growled. He was fierce and angry, but Coyote ran away before Badger could rip him to shreds. Coyote went about telling everyone that Badger carried bad medicine, but the truth was that Coyote simply didn't understand the darkness. Now, Badger is a powerful totem who can be a protector, keeping the dark energies at bay, but his medicine is difficult to carry. If it is not balanced with Deer, life can be sad and lonely, for Badger out of control is feared and hated. But there are many people for whom a touch of Badger is just the right medicine: people who need some self-respect, the courage to say No when enough is enough, the strength to act on what is important to them, to seize opportunities and make changes in their lives."

Ashton's regular voice came back, close and soft, as he continued, "So that's what the Lord of the Animals said to me, and then he touched the side of my head. I woke up to find myself lying in the yard, with Norbert and Ray's badger a few feet away, eating my ear. He had taken it for restitution. Payback for the prairie dogs. There was no malice. He was pure. And now, so was I."

I must have looked sick. He quickly covered the ear again. "And here's the best part—with my left ear I can hear things that are...well, beyond this plane. Outside this sphere."

I suddenly had an intense desire to get up and walk away, but the desire to wilt, to just stay where I sat, seemed even stronger. I can only guess at what was on my face. He smiled and kept talking.

"It's kind of like music, or maybe a breeze in the aspens. Sometimes it reminds me of the whistle of a bull elk, or deeper, like a foghorn in a storm. Or it crashes like waves, sort of a symphony of waves. Mostly it's a tiny whisper or tinkle of sound, as if someone touched a silver spoon to a crystal goblet out in the airless darkness of cold space. It's like radar. I track it, tune it in, and follow my path. Nothing is a surprise. I hear the song of it before it happens. But I don't always know what the song means until the instant its physical manifestation hits my sight. So I try to keep my doors of perception cleansed, to paraphrase Blake."

On and on his voice went. The alarm I felt was real, but it was faint, and growing fainter. Somehow, I couldn't wake my critical mind. I wanted to, but I couldn't make myself believe he was crazy. That's why I felt I could say, "You're crazy, man."

"Of course, if you really thought so, you'd be gone by now. So let me tell you something else I know: this is a very important night for both of us." I shivered. He laughed. My eyelids wanted desperately to close. I dragged my forearm slowly to the tabletop so I could see my wristwatch. It was midnight.

That's when the lights went out.

Lightning flashed, thunder cracked, and the diner was instantly in utter blackness. There was a palpable sensation of absence in the air, a sort of death as all electrical vibration in the city ceased in one instant. Not a glimmer of light came in the windows; surely, car headlights passed by outside, but I don't remember being aware of even the faintest hint of luminance. The things I remember best from the midst of that darkness are these: the warm pressure of Ashton's hand as it came to rest on my forearm, and the sound of his voice, a soft deep whisper in my ear. It's as if I still feel the imprint of both those touches on my flesh, even all these hours later. I don't even know what he was saying, but it seems he was telling a story of rolling sage-covered prairies dotted by stands of shivering gold aspens, with blue mountain peaks in the distance, growing ever nearer, slowly, oh so slowly. And his hand was strong, a pressure that held me in my seat even as I heard other sounds, sounds that seemed far away even though they were so close they stopped my breath and made my heart flop crazily.

It was as if I dreamed. I heard the sounds of bodies in struggle. I heard the crash of falling objects. I heard Felicity cry out, first in fear, then in pain. I heard Achmed's guttural laugh, his hoarse breathing. And I heard his breath stop abruptly, with a sickening silence. And all the while Ashton's hand held my arm; all the while Ashton's voice whispered, whispered, whispered in my ear.

Then, after who knows how long, there was a surge of audible energy in the air, and all the lights came back on. I was alone in the booth. I sat for a while trying to gather my dull wits. Ashton was gone. Everyone was gone. It seemed I was alone in the diner, until I heard sniffling and saw Felicity rise up from behind the counter, hair awry, makeup smeared, clutching her torn shirt around her breasts, and wiping blood from her nose.

Around the counter, everything was in a shambles, utensils and broken dishes strewn on the floor, cake smeared across several stools, napkins everywhere. There was no sign of Achmed, nor of Ashton.

"Are you hurt bad?" I asked.

"No. I'll be fine." Ducking her head, she hurried toward the restroom in the back. I began picking up some of the broken dishes, feeling as if I was waking up from a drugged nightmare.

"I guess we better call the cops. And shouldn't you go to a hospital or something?" I said when she came out again.

She refused both. "Thank you for helping," she said. "But I can finish up now. Just gotta lock the door so nobody can come in."

"I feel stupid asking this, but what just happened?"

Her mouth trembled a moment, and a flicker of panic went through her eyes. She seemed unsure of how to answer, at first genuinely confused, then mustering up a streetwise show of cool. "I don't want to talk about it," she said, and turned away from me to clean up a spilled dessert. "But tell your friend thank you, okay?"

I couldn't get her to say more. And still there was no sign of either Achmed or Ashton. I helped out a little more, but gradually everything seemed to be returning to something resembling normal in the Tunnel Diner. I was even feeling awake again, the coffee pumping in my veins, and my watch showed it was after one a.m., so I told Felicity goodbye and drove away into the rain.

I pulled into my driveway after almost an hour of growing dread, dread aggravated by my feeling of stupid bewilderment about the circumstances of the evening. I knew something was wrong even before I tried my key in the lock and it didn't work. Then I noticed the note taped to the door. It was not hard to read in the glare of the porch light, but the bugs swarming the bulb sent crazy shadows flitting across the page. The note was typewritten but signed by Ann with her full name. It told me that she had had the locks changed at midnight. She was divorcing me, citing adultery and mental cruelty. If I tried to enter the house, she would call the police and demand a restraining order. And I was not to leave town until I had committed to a suitable amount of alimony and child support.

Even in the typed text, I could hear her voice: the belligerence that shocked me every time, the fragile desperation masked so often by threats she could never back up. The inexplicable hatred.

I stood there on the silent, shadowy porch for a long, stunned minute, then I left.

I GOT THIS MOTEL room with the mistaken idea that I could get a few hours of sleep. Ha. Everything I've built my life around, my marriage, my family, it's all crumbling. Of course I can't sleep, who could? Yet in the wee hours of the night, I found myself obsessing, not about Ann, but about the events in the diner. I even dredged up the Mormon mythology I learned as a child but had long since left behind: maybe Ashton Gill was one of the "Three Nephites," sort of Mormon Bodhisattvas, three righteous men from an ancient American civilization of Hebrew immigrants whose descendants became the American Indians. These three men were so good that when offered eternal salvation, they chose instead to wander the earth forever, using their magical powers to help others get to heaven. Could it be true? All of it? Should I have stayed a faithful Mormon, and would that have saved my family? No. There is no answer.

So here I am, wide awake but feeling trembly with exhaustion, as the sun begins to peek around the curtains. I thought that by writing about it, I could make sense of all this, but now I know: I can't explain anything that happened in the Tunnel Diner. At first, I was frustrated by that. Now, maybe not. The more I meditated on all this, this Mystery with a capital M, as I paced and sat, swimming in the weird displacement of these hours in the belly of the night...the more I considered the dull explicability of my life until now...the more I pondered the endlessness behind the wall of blue above us...the more I surrendered, the more I began to feel in love with the Question. I can never explain this night, and therefore I am free.

I don't know what will happen in the day that is dawning, and the days after that. Surely there will be much pain, but right now I feel strong, not in my body but in my heart. I can embrace the changes roaring toward me, and I can make other changes, the ones that need to be made. I am a man. I can be the man I want to be.

So I am going to cock one ear toward the ground, and the other toward the sky, and I'm going to listen with all my mind and heart. There may be whispers meant just for me. And Ashton Gill I will never forget. I will wonder about him from time to time. I will always hope he made it to the Center, and beyond. And I am glad that I have his handwriting here with me: a souvenir of the adventure that just began and will not end until I die. Just now, I reached into my jacket pocket and found a diner napkin that held, in a graceful scribble, this note:

"Jeff, my friend— a Chippewa medicine woman once said:
Sometimes I go about pitying myself,
And all the time
I am being carried on great winds across the sky."

B.4 Another Dream

I STAND ON A rocky bluff at dusk, next to an ancient pine. At my feet, a man's dead body, red plaid, blue jeans, face turned away. It's my job to stand guard, but I'm afraid to see his face. The view below is a lake so deep it's black. On the distant shore, glassy skyscrapers bend in the wind like palms.

Dreams are like fiction: they lie to tell the truth. But which dreams are mine? And which parts are lies?

B.5 A Perfect June

NOW THAT SCHOOL WAS out for the summer, Brandt was working Saturdays at the motel as well as helping with his father's carpet-laying business during the week. He had expected that sending the stolen story out into the world would lift it from his thoughts; after all, he had no high expectations for winning the contest. Instead, the story's absence had the opposite effect on him. Like a parent whose child is away from home for the first time, he found himself obsessing about "The Tunnel Diner." He marveled at the way he remembered everything so intimately; he didn't need to read the story—it was all there, fully alive in his memory. Not as words on a page, but as sensory experience: color, aroma, texture, sound, even emotion. In his recollection, he *was* Jimmy Campbell, or rather Jeff Carter, living the events in the story. But one thing was missing—or more precisely, it was there, but frustratingly just out of reach—and that was the face of Molly. No, not Molly. Ann.

Mere days into the summer break, Brandt's attention had been captured, along with the world's, by the massacre of students at Tiananmen Square. He had been aware of the uprising that had been going on since April and felt a vague solidarity, along with a shadow of middle-class shame. He hoped he would have the guts to stand up against injustice if ever he were actually faced with it, but he knew chances were slim that spoiled young Americans would be driven to any such action in the foreseeable future. As he watched the video clip of a lone man facing down a column of tanks, he was surprised to feel tears suddenly spring to his eyes. Such courage was mind-boggling and heart-wrenching. But there was something else...the way the man stood, face to face with the giant machinery of death, it was as if he were looking into a mirror. He was a slim, white-shirted Everyman carrying a shopping bag, contemplating, in front of millions, the fearsome darkness in the human soul. In his own soul. Staring it down, or perhaps coming to an understanding of it. And then he was gone.

That scene was replayed in more than one conversation at a school's-out party Brandt attended, everyone abuzz, but he found he didn't really want to discuss it. There was just too much in his head that he couldn't begin to articulate. He was filling his plastic cup from the keg for a second time when he felt a warm breath in his ear.

"Hi there, mister writer." Her sultry whisper almost made him laugh; clearly, she was ahead of him on the beers. Patti Ann Porter had been, briefly, his high school love. Even now there was a twinge of pain as he faced her and experienced the familiar rush of overlapping memories: the two of them losing their virginity together in her girlish bedroom, the fumbling, the freckles on her breasts, the incredible deliciousness, and then the beginnings of an actual sexual relationship, two more times, better each time he thought, but then her inexplicable avoidance, and the tearful end, both of them crying, so embarrassing. She had told him she was unhappy, that he was emotionally immature, couldn't express his feelings, and she felt shut out, unloved. He retreated, hid, they didn't speak for months, and then finally were cordial friends, as if it were all a dream.

"Hey, Patti Ann...so how's NYU?"

"I heard about you. You wrote a story that got some professor all excited. That is just so...so fucking cool." Her body tilted toward him and she put her hand on his chest.

He felt embarrassed. "Well...not really." She was so inviting, her green eyes looking up at him through that ever-present front lock, a copper-colored veil, but the soft slur in her voice reminded him of the only other time he had had sex in the two-plus years since they broke up. At another party, he had found himself in a strange bedroom with a girl whose name he didn't know, a girl who was so drunk he suspected she thought he was someone else entirely, but he let her put her tongue in his mouth and her hand in his pants, and they went all the way in a liquid blur, and it felt nothing like it had felt with Patti Ann.

"Jay McInerney came and spoke to one of my classes. I think he reminded me of you." Her hand slid down his chest to his belly.

Brandt had no idea who she was talking about, and he didn't care. He was suddenly very aware of a mix of impulses: one, to kiss her, and two, to push her away. The weird part of number two was that the reason he wanted to push her away was that he sensed, hovering just outside the range of his mind's eye, the blurry presence of Molly. Another man's wife, an older woman, a mother, a person he'd never met. The feeling was that no matter how much his secret heart yearned to hold his first love close again, he couldn't do it. He couldn't be unfaithful to Molly; he didn't want to betray her.

Something was definitely wrong here.

"Brandt! *License to Kill*, man—next month!" It was the loud voice of an old high-school teammate, Jason Black, approaching with Kumar. "Timothy Dalton again. Let's go see it, man!"

Brandt was aware of Patti Ann's hand on his stomach as he shrugged, "Ehh, maybe. There's no such novel by Fleming, y'know. This is just Hollywood gone wild." He had no interest in the new Bond movie, and he observed himself having no interest. But he couldn't stay here with Patti Ann, her arm touching his, her head so near his shoulder. He reached around her with his free hand, gave her shoulders a squeeze and her head a kiss, and disentangled.

"See you later, Patti Ann." He took his full cup of beer and followed Jason and Kumar to another room.

The month of June ticked along, green and beautiful, temperatures perfect, a surprising number of pure blue skies. Brandt did little but work. Occasionally in the evenings, he and Kumar would catch a movie or drive aimlessly from town to town, talking about girls they knew or wished they knew. With every day that passed, Brandt spent more time rolling like a marble between his fingers the feeling of being inhabited by Jimmy Campbell. The alien concerns of family, bills, job, even home repairs and yard work, seemed to loom just above his head in an invisible cloud. His body felt different: bigger, more burdensome. He found himself worrying about Molly, his "wife." He wondered, why am I worrying? But then a nebulous impression of two children, their small bodies, oddly faceless, squirming in his arms, would make him smile.

Foreign images and sensations began to interrupt whatever he was doing. He was unable to stop the thoughts. When he tried, with a stern command as if his mind were a dog in training, for a moment all would return to its old familiar Brandt-ness. Still, it was never more than a few minutes before the beast had, without his realizing it, pulled him by the leash back into forbidden territory.

One morning at the motel, he pulled out the telephone directory again and found the listing for A.J. Campbell. He wrote down the address and the phone number. When his shift was over that afternoon, he drove to Sparta and found the mock Tudor where the Campbells had once been a happy family. He cruised slowly past it, back and forth, then parked a few car-lengths away and sat staring at the house.

In the front yard, parked neatly side by side, were a tiny blue tricycle and a miniature pink bike with training wheels. He sat for several minutes, inert, taking in the details of this home, its neat ordinariness, the dark beams and pale stucco, the shrubbery screening the front stoop, the garden hose coiled on a hook by the driveway, the slightly overgrown lawn. He wondered what strange thing he would do next. As he watched, a Toyota station wagon came from behind him and turned into the Campbells' driveway. A pretty young woman with long, straight blonde hair and slim-cut jeans got out of the driver's door. She came around the back of the car, and he had an impulse to duck down and hide. But no need; her attention was on the children. She didn't see him as she opened the door and leaned in to unbuckle safety belts and let two miniature versions of herself come bounding from the car, the girl taller with longer hair, both of them in shorts and t-shirts and sneakers, and both in constant jumpy motion, with small voices clamoring nonsense. The kids ran to the front door as their mother picked up a grocery bag from the front seat. In the slanting late afternoon sunlight, she tossed her hair in a golden arc as she stood up straight, and it was as if she were in slow motion as she walked toward the house with a graceful, athletic stride, her laugh ringing out.

Brandt was aroused. It all came on in an instant: something new for him, something about her motherhood: that she was a woman, not a girl; an experienced adult, not a silly virgin. But at the same time, she was young and fit and beautiful. He was stunned. He wanted her.

Molly Campbell and her kids disappeared into the house. Brandt took a deep breath and tried to calm his rushing blood. He spoke sternly to himself: *this is not good, this is trouble, drive away now.* He reasoned with himself: *Don't be stupid. Don't be a creep. To pursue another man's wife is not only foolish, it's immoral. Who are you? Who have you become?*

Brandt thought about his parents. His dad was a good guy, a small businessman who tried to give quality service to his customers at a fair price. He liked jazz and corny puns. He had become so profoundly sad when his wife died, Brandt had wondered if the man would ever smile again.

And his mother...his mother was more complicated. She had been known by everyone to be a sweet person, a kind person. Bright flowers were always on the table and cheerful slogans on the refrigerator. Only Brandt and his father ever saw the churning darkness she kept so well hidden, the rage that showed in the tightening of lips, the narrowing of eyes, and then the bitter sarcasm, all triggered by seeming irrelevancies. But she had always worked hard at being what she hoped was a good person, and then she got sick, and that was the end.

Brandt knew that he loved these people. He would never want to disappoint them.

He reached up and twisted the rear-view mirror so he could look at himself, look directly into his own eyes. But there was nothing new there. No big truth to confront. Two familiar brown eyes just stared back at him from the rectangle of glass, a fragment, not a whole face. Not whole, and with everything backward: the lie of mirrors, all features flipped, not the way others see us at all, but the only way we can ever see ourselves in the current moment. Backwards.

It was a perfect summer day sliding toward dusk, the blue sky in the east just a shade deeper, and shadows starting to stretch long across the suburban lawns. Brandt opened the car door, swung out and up, stood to his full height, and let the door fall shut behind him. He stood for the length of two breaths. Then he walked across the street, straight toward the Campbell family's front door.

C. The Photographer

C.1 A Familiar Face

FOR THE NEXT FEW weeks of A.J.'s life, everything seemed almost normal, as if Robbie Brand had been nothing more than a bit of blur in the eye: a few blinks and he was gone.

During the first week, A.J. made a quick follow-up call to the editor at *Espresso Lit* and learned that she had indeed told Brand that A.J. wanted to speak to him; beyond that, there was nothing she could do. Then she added an afterthought: A.J. should keep an eye out for other publications, or maybe even readings, by Brand. ..because there were sure to be some, and maybe there would be an opportunity to meet him at some point. From this A.J. reasoned that there was a very good chance Brand was in New York, and he promised himself to stay alert to the local literary scene.

That same day, A.J. repeated his frequent trek up Sixth Avenue to 20th Street, right turn at the Limelight disco church, and down the block to Duggal Labs. He picked up the slides from his late-night photo shoot, opened the package immediately, and spread them out on a light table in the lobby. A few were duds, but most looked reasonably well-exposed and seemed to capture the effects he'd been trying for. With a loupe, he peered closely at a few of the more promising candidates, and one in particular, but he couldn't be sure if any were perfect without seeing them projected large. He decided he'd get around to that task sometime later; he had no money to get prints made anyway, so the decision could wait. With that, his thoughts turned back to the routine of earning a living and seeing his kids, punctuated occasionally by his usual interests, including a video project of his own invention. And movies, always movies.

The Quad on 13th Street was playing a documentary he'd heard was good: *Let's Get Lost*, the film by Bruce Weber about jazz trumpeter Chet Baker. Several nights later, he strolled the few blocks alone and settled into a front and center seat in one of the small theaters, not knowing what to expect.

A.J. was not a music sophisticate. He knew next to nothing about jazz. He knew pop songs from the radio, but beyond that, his only studious listening had been to a few early Bob Dylan records long ago, at first to keep up with the retro-cool style of a few film majors at college, but then with a sincere appreciation he'd shared with his wife in their early years together. He had wanted to see the Chet Baker film for its photography, and he was not disappointed. He loved the moody black-and-white look of the film, its camera motion, lighting, editing—all seeming so free-wheeling but at the same time so beautifully controlled.

He loved the photography, but the music is what surprised him most. More than once he was moved nearly to tears by Baker's dreamy minor-key trumpet and languid, whispery vocals, all of it smoky, sexy, hypnotic, a little dangerous. When the movie ended, he sat slumped far down in his seat past the final credits, then stood up and walked out into the night, striding east to Broadway, then straight downtown to 4th Street and Tower Records.

In the jazz stacks upstairs, he found the *Let's Get Lost* soundtrack CD. The pale, emaciated kid with bright eyes and spiky hair who helped him said, "Hey man, if you like this, I wanna turn you on to somethin' else too...." He beckoned for A.J. to follow as he kept talking. "A little on the weird side like Chet, but hey, we're into that, right?" He took A.J. to the folk section and pulled out a CD called *Lorca* by Tim Buckley. "Really, try it."

A.J. was not accustomed to spending freely but before he left the store he'd added Nick Drake's *Pink Moon* and the Miles Davis classics *Kind of Blue* and *In a Silent Way*.

That night as he listened, he wondered about himself, his taste for this dark and dreamy stuff. Heroin music. Why was this what he was drawn to?

THREE WEEKS AND A paycheck later, on a rainy evening, A.J. stayed in his apartment, opened a beer, and put the soundtrack of *Let's Get Lost* on his little boombox. He tacked a big sheet of poster board to the wall, found the packet of Sixth Avenue slides, and set up his projector with a stack loader rather than a carousel. He turned out the overhead light and advanced through the slides one by one, looking carefully at each, making notes of which were most successful. Nearing the end of the stack, he came to the one he had thought was best. Yes, it had the perfect blend of streaked motion and crisp color, but it was ruined by a passerby—a guy standing on the sidewalk, looking directly at the camera.

A.J. cursed aloud. He hadn't noticed the guy at all when he shot the photo. He took a closer look at the image on the wall. The man was standing still, with a direct, expressionless stare—eye contact with A.J. His body was partially transparent due to the long exposure, but his face was clear. At his side, holding his hand, was a dark-haired child, blurred and shadowy. Gradually, a chilling prickle of familiarity crept up A.J.'s neck. He leaned even closer to the projection and inspected the man's face. Yes, it had to be him: Ashton Gill, the hitchhiker he'd encountered in the Tunnel Diner years ago.

Damn! Was I blind? I've wanted to speak to him again, A.J. thought. But now, it was as if the photograph proved that Gill was even more a phantom than ever...right here in the Village but out of reach, an illusion, insubstantial as mist.

In the same month, two inexplicable visitations from his past—the "Desert Vacation" story and now this. How could they not be related? Maybe Ashton Gill was Robbie Brand. He groaned. More detective work was required.

The following Saturday morning was hazy and promised a hot, muggy day. Summer in New York City had begun. A.J. strolled to the library again and repeated the tedious sleuthing activities he'd pursued for Robbie Brand, but with even fewer results. He found census records of two men whose middle and last names were Ashton Gill, but one had to be near ninety and the other long dead, both from the South. There was a woman, Ashton Marie, apparently in Texas. A matronly librarian told A.J. that, to find a person, the library was just not the best place to look. There were many other sources of information: licensed computer databases, court records, tax records, more—all tools that cops and private investigators would use. Searching those would take not only money, but lots of time. He was no PI. His enthusiasm couldn't survive. As far as he could tell, the man he was looking for did not exist.

Once again, he surrendered to his own powerlessness in the face of mystery. He vowed to just keep his eyes open for what would happen next.

What happened next was that he had an idea. He thought of his friend Felicity, with whom he'd kept in touch ever since they shared that strange midnight experience in the diner where she worked. Her birthday was coming up soon. The image with Ashton Gill in it, framed for her wall, would make a great gift. It was beautiful, it was art by a friend, and it contained what seemed to be the face of her long-ago benefactor, the man who had saved her from an ugly assault. His eye contact with the camera made it even more personal.

A.J. returned to his apartment, put the slide into an envelope, and walked in the sweaty humidity up Sixth Avenue to Duggal Labs.

C.2 The Split

WORK HAD SLOWED A bit and A.J. was glad for the opportunity to forge ahead on the art project he'd conjured up out of a fragmentary dream he'd had months ago. The details of the dream were lost to his memory, replaced by the thing he was creating in an attempt to capture the dream's feeling. It was a bit of experimental video-making that he was calling "The Split."

Nick Pappas was willing to work for no pay on the shooting day and bring along the camera and sound gear that he owned. Mitchell Frank, a young actor who'd worked on one of the Image Impact Inc. corporate shoots, was happy to donate his time on an artsy production that would show off his thespian skills. To finish up the project, A.J. had arranged for some free Sunday hours on the editing system owned by his friends at I.I.I.

A.J.'s apartment was magically transformed into a cramped but sufficient studio for the simple shoot. He had planned it all very carefully. Window light was blocked out, and on one wall they hung an eight-foot-wide swath of heavy black paper pulled from a roll. They put the camera on a tripod as near to the opposite wall as possible. The lighting setup used small units on lightweight stands in a basic three-point scheme, with various colored gels to change mood. Seated in a chair in the center, Mitchell appeared in the viewfinder in a medium close-up in black limbo. He was to speak directly to the camera, nothing more.

The apartment felt dark with a bright center, like a cave with a campfire. A.J. was behind the camera. As well as handling the sound recording, Nick operated a small teleprompter system. The scrolling script was reflected in a two-way mirror that hung at a slant across the front of the camera. The lens, an invisible eye, peered through the mirror to record its subject. Mitchell could read his lines and act his dual role, while keeping eye contact with the camera—that is, with the eventual viewer, the absent audience, the other participant in an imaginary dialogue.

They recorded the full five-minute script twice, once for each of Mitchell's two characters. He was a skilled actor and understood

A.J.'s directions about emotional tone and mood shift; the lack of preparation and rehearsal never became a problem. With pauses to change colors on the lights, and with a few false starts and retakes, the whole thing, setup to wrap, took four hours. A.J. was as happy as he'd felt in years. He took the guys out for a beer and dinner at Benny's Burritos, and then got a good night's sleep.

At 6:00 the next morning he went into post-production. Using the key he'd borrowed, he let himself into the little two-room suite that I.I.I. inhabited on weekdays, three flights up in a Hell's Kitchen pre-war factory converted to offices. He had spent most of a previous Saturday learning the basics of the Media 100 computer system and now he methodically went about the digitizing and sequencing of his chosen takes, following the notes he'd written. The split-screen effect he'd planned took some trial and error, but he was eventually satisfied with the result. By 11:00 he had constructed half the video, but he had to stop. It was time to head for New Jersey to spend the afternoon and evening with his kids.

As he copied the work-in-progress to a video cassette to take with him, he sat back and watched it, pretending to be detached, pretending to be someone else.

The image faded in from blackness. The screen was divided in half, each half delineated by an identical ornate gold frame, as if two portraits or two mirrors were side by side. In each was a close-up of Mitchell, his angular features warmly lit and his light brown hair catching highlights. To A.J., they were simply ONE and TWO. The face on the left spoke first.

ONE *(a bit dreamy)*: My eye is a camera. My eye....
TWO *(interrupting, with a smile)*: Mind's eye, third eye, eye of the needle, window of the soul....

ONE: ...is a camera. It was always this way.... *(In reverie now, as if seeing a vision.)* She sits across the little table from me, framed in a rectangle etched on my vision like on a ground glass. Fine lines, crosshairs in a circle, delicately trace the center of my sight....

TWO *(interrupting again, his smile more sardonic)*: Insight, foresight, second sight, a sight for sore eyes...

ONE *(his voice stays soft and he never acknowledges TWO)*: The street lamp sends a blue kicker slanting across black hair, tracing her left cheek. A limo cruising Bleecker Street washes a pale fill light across her face, sparkling a split second in those dark eyes. Her golden key light, thick and rich as the aroma of fresh Italian bread, spills from the window of the bakery on her right. My left. Camera left. It was always this way, since my earliest memory....

TWO *(his smile has grown cruel)*: Digital, random-access, read-only memory. An elephant's memory. Ha!

(During the following, TWO grows visibly impatient.)

ONE: When she shifts her weight, leans a little, looks to the right or left, I make the necessary adjustments. Pan right ever so sl ightly...tilt up a fraction of an inch...keep her framed in a nice close-up, not too much headroom. Watch the dynamics...the way the curving line of her shoulder intersects the frame edge, the way the shifting angle of her head changes the negative space. Move with the shot, flow like water, keep it balanced, keep it composed. Keep it beautiful.

(ONE suddenly fades to black and TWO is bathed in red light. During the following, ONE very slowly fades up again.)

TWO *(manic, gesticulating, his voice harsh)*: Cut! Print it! Ha ha! Another piece of celluloid illusion in the can! Get that goddamned dolly track out of the way! Dismantle this shit! Amber gels off the 5-K in the bakery set! Blue off the junior! Send the limo home, he's finished! Sophia, baby, that was nice, keep it up! Who the hell is *that* guy? If he's a grip, tell him to get off his ass, we're on to the next set-up! I want heavy pink and gold on that entire bank of HMI's! And wash the whole cyc with that Rosco full blue, and add a little opal! It's gotta be indigo! Indigo! Move, move, move! This ain't foreplay here!

(TWO suddenly fades to black and ONE is now lit in soft pink with a blue accent.)

ONE: Last week I was walking the edge of the Hudson. Jersey side. It was twilight. The moon was rising, full and pink, hanging in indigo among the dazzling golden towers of lower Manhattan. All was silent there, across the water. Flickering across my vision....

TWO *(suddenly appearing)*: Television!

ONE: ...overlaid like images from a digital frame-store device....

TWO *(with a sneer)*: Prisoner of his own device!

ONE: ...came pictures of silent sandstone walls and towers, an empty desert, brick-red under a rising moon. Ancient spirits were whispering in the blue shadows of the canyons....

Black. That was it, as far as he got. For a moment, A.J. sat still and mused: *Okay, so some people will call it gimmicky and pretentious. I don't care.* Then he stuffed the camera master tape and the VHS edited copy in his backpack, locked the door behind him and clattered down the stairs. He felt great. The whole thing was going so perfectly, he could not have imagined the project would never be finished.

C.3 Modern Family

The day was humid and hot, and his old Toyota had no air conditioning. Pilar from the Supervised Visitation Network sat in the
passenger seat, his kids in the back, the breeze blowing everyone's
hair. They were on their way to a destination he had picked for
its beauty and, he hoped, its cooler temperatures: Tillman Ravine.
Part of a State Forest, it was a lovely trail along a cascading brook
in woods dense with ferns and mossy stone ledges, an intensely
green place his old Utah self could never have imagined existed
in New Jersey. He had once thought "Garden State" must be a
joke, but living in the northwest corner of the state soon taught
him otherwise. The ravine was only a half-hour drive from their
former home in Sparta and had become an occasional refuge for
him that last painful summer of marriage. He wanted to share it
with his kids now that they were old enough to appreciate natural
beauty. He imagined them loving it there, singing along the trail,
leaping fallen logs, spying minnows in the pools, laughing as they
picnicked on a giant flat boulder, then riding home exhausted,
rosy-cheeked and sleepy.

"This is a stupid car," Lizzie said.

"What?" he said loudly over the wind in his ears.

"Your car is stupid!" she shouted. "You should get a new one
with air conditioning!"

"Lizzie..." he began, aware as always that his every word and
gesture was being observed and judged. "Come on...this is a good
car."

"It's a piece of junk! Mom says it's probably not safe."

"Well, it *is* safe. Don't you worry."

Usually quiet, Max spoke up with a drawn-out whine. "I'm too hot."

"I know, buddy. But really, you're too old to whine like that. We'll be there soon. The stream and the shade make it cooler there. You'll see."

"I hope you're right," Pilar said, barely loud enough for him to hear.

A.J. parked next to several other cars at the trailhead. Max was the first one out of the car, happy to have outgrown his booster seat. A.J. was glad to see him grin and hop in place like a pogo stick as he looked at the trail disappearing into shady woods. Pilar opened Lizzie's door, but Lizzie refused to unfasten her seat belt. Her arms were folded and her face set in an exaggerated scowl.

"This place is stupid," she said.

"It's nice and cool here," A.J. said, and immediately regretted it. The truth was, it was damned hot, and everybody knew it.

"I hate hikes," Lizzie said. Max stared at her and said nothing.

"Look in here," A.J said, pulling a backpack out of the car's trunk and unzipping it. "See, sandwiches and chips and soda. We're gonna have a picnic by the water. It'll be fun!" He heard a faint sigh from Pilar.

"I *hate* picnics!" Lizzie yelled.

"I'm too hot," Max repeated with the same grating whine.

A.J. felt the cheery edifice he'd been propping up inside himself crumble. Why have hopes, why imagine sweet family scenes, why bother? He didn't know whether he was sad or angry, but he knew he could show neither. He glanced at Pilar, who shrugged.

He sat down on the gravel next to the open car door, took a deep breath, and let it out slowly. "Okay, you guys, how about this...forget the hike. We'll eat our picnic in the car while we drive. Let's go visit Felicity and Bernard, whadya say?"

"I hate that kid. He's weird," Lizzie said. But her scowl had relaxed.

"Yeah," said Max.

"He's not weird, he just can't speak." A.J. said. Felicity's son Bernard was mute for reasons no one had yet figured out.

"He thinks he's funny, but he's just stupid. He's a total retard."

"Lizzie, stop now!"

"Plus, he's way older than us, Dad. He's a teenager, and we're just innocent little kids who need to be protected! Right, Pilar?"

Pilar said, "Don't try to get me involved, Elizabeth."

A.J. wiped sweat from his forehead, feeling overloaded. "Thank you."

Lizzie continued, "And anyway, we want to go to *The Lion King*."

"Yeah!" said Max, and he pogo-hopped. "Lion King!"

Three hours later, they were sitting in Rockaway Mall eating ice cream cones. A.J. had to admit that he had enjoyed the movie and the relief from the outdoor furnace. Even Pilar was smiling.

"So...let's talk about it," A.J. said as they were finishing their cones. "Simba was out there with those silly little guys and he forgot who he was, right?"

"Hakuna matata!" Max sang. He jumped off his stool and began dancing. Lizzie joined in, "Hakuna matata, hakuna matata!" A.J. and Pilar clapped rhythm while the kids danced and repeated the refrain to the point of utter insufferableness.

"Okay," A.J. said, "Let's talk. So, he forgot who he was. What should he have done?"

Lizzie gave a loud sigh and rolled her eyes. Max licked ice cream off his fingers.

A.J. kept at it. "Here's what I think. He needed to keep asking himself the very important question, 'Who am I?'"

"Dad, you're such a loser," Lizzie said.

BACK AT MOLLY'S HOUSE, the entirely renovated, multi-gabled Victorian in Morristown that she'd bought with her inheritance, a Mercedes convertible sat in the driveway behind Molly's Honda minivan.

"Whose car is that?" A.J. said, directing the question to Pilar, whose plain Chevy sat at the curb.

"None of my business," she said as she got out.

"Richard," Max said.

Lizzie said, "Shh!"

A.J. and Molly had long since let go of the formal visitation handoff, but he was curious, so he followed the kids through the front door and into the shady, earth-toned coolness of the living room.

"Mom, we went to The Lion King!" Max shouted, as Lizzie threw herself onto the wide leather couch like a sullen teenager.

"No need to yell, I'm right here," said Molly as she came in from the kitchen. She wore a white tennis outfit and carried a glass of white wine. Behind her, in matching whites and with a matching drink, came Richard: handsome, trim, and tan. *Goddamned cliché*, thought A.J.

Molly wore her hair in a trendy bob now. She stopped, startled, when she saw A.J. He watched as her face hardened to a sneering mask. "So," she said. "If it isn't the famous writer, Robbie Brand."

"What?" Nothing could have been less expected. A.J. was speechless.

"You can't just publish our family details because you feel like it, Jimmy. Richard's a lawyer. I can sue you."

"What on earth are you talking about?"

"Don't do the innocent act. Right there on the coffee table—all the evidence I need."

A.J. sat heavily on the couch next to Lizzie and picked up a thin magazine from a group spread out on the polished mahogany. It appeared to be an avant-garde art thing with the title *Hades Twist*. He opened it to a middle page marked by a ragged-edged strip of yellow note paper. At the top of the page was a title: "Dylan Time," and an author's name: Robbie Brand. A.J. scanned the first paragraph—enough to see what he had feared. The story was about him, him and Molly. He closed the book and picked up another, *Pratfall* it was called, turning to the page with the yellow bookmark: "The Tunnel Diner" by Robbie Brand. Again, he could see within a few sentences where it was going, and he closed the book. Then he saw the folded newsprint and the masthead, *Espresso Lit*, and he knew that "Desert Vacation" was inside that one. Several other slender books sported ragged yellow strips marking pages where he knew he'd find new violations.

"You!" he said, jumping to his feet, his finger in her face. "You always said offense was the best defense! You're trying to turn this on me. It's you! *You're* Robbie Brand!"

Richard stepped forward. "Hey, now—"

Molly laughed and tossed her blond bob. "Ha! As if I would ever bother to do all this work. For what?" She laughed again. "Really, what purpose? Money?"

Lizzie laughed with her. "Come on, Dad. Admit it. You're busted."

Even Max chimed in, hopping as he cackled, "Dad's busted, Dad's busted!"

Richard was smiling too. Now Molly tilted her head to one side and put on an exaggerated maternal tone. "Jimmy, are you really so desperate? Pay the rent with our family secrets?"

A.J. felt his face burn. He was boiling inside, muscles rigid. "I didn't write this stuff!"

Richard started, "Denials aren't— "

A.J. cut him off: "You stay out of it." Then to Molly: "I saw one of these stories too and I've been trying to find the author. But I didn't know about the others. Where did you get these?"

Lizzie answered with a put-on theatrical voice and an out-flung arm. "Why, Jimmy, you sent them in the mail! What, you forgot? Oh, my! Or are you still lying, Dad?"

Max was twirling in circles now. "Yeah, Dad Dad Dad Dad!"

"That's enough out of both of you!" A.J. yelled. "This is not a discussion you should even be involved in."

Molly snapped, "You're in *my* house now, Jimmy. Watch your tone." Lizzie put her nose in the air and waggled her head. Max flopped into a chair and closed his eyes.

A.J. took a deep breath. An errant ray from the setting sun made a leafy pattern on the wall behind Molly. "Look…I swear I didn't write this stuff. I've been looking for the guy for weeks. I thought maybe somebody stole my journals, or…I don't know what. But now I really want to read all of it so I can figure out what's going on here. Can I take these with me?"

Molly laughed again with a hair toss. "No way! Why would I—"

Richard interrupted. "Actually, Mol, I've written down all the particulars, each magazine issue, title, page number. Even some notes about the content. So, in good faith, let's let him take these, with a promise to return them. See what happens."

Molly looked surprised and not at all pleased to have her power position undercut. "Well...okay then, if that's your official advice." Then, to A.J.: "But don't destroy them, or I swear—"

"I won't! Why would I?" A.J. gathered up the armful of journals. "I'll be in touch."

He left without another word, not even to his offspring, those little vermin. Enough was enough.

C.4 "Dylan Time," a Short Story by Robbie Brand

In Hades Twist, *this story was prefaced by the following: "Editor's Note: The legal apparatus of the large corporation that is Bob Dylan presented this writer with insurmountable financial obstacles in the interest of maximizing their own revenue (of which, apparently, they don't have enough). Song lyrics are therefore redacted, which offers not only a whimsical guessing game, but also an interesting pattern on the page. Just what we like."*

BEFORE MY DIVORCE, IN the window of years between the births of my two children, there was a brief, shimmering moment when my wife and I once again found our love for each other. It only lasted about six months, but its echo continues, down through all the years since. Back then, we called it "Dylan Time."

It started when our daughter was over a year old and could finally sleep through the night, occasionally. One evening after Annie and I had furtively made love and were lying together in silence, I saw in my peripheral vision a lock of my own longish, dull-yellow hair mixing with her waterfall of pale gold tresses. For a second, I had a vision of us as if from a camera across the room, our nakedness in an amber glow like a softcore movie. I said, "Wow—blonde on blonde."

I got up from the bed, leafed through my old albums in the living room, and put Dylan's 1966 classic on the turntable, volume low so as not to wake Lily. Annie and I lay together in the semi-dark, naked limbs entwined, and listened to the whole double album, starting with the raucous "Rainy Day Women…" and on through all the rest of it, the jangly folk rock, the crazy flood of lyrics. Something about that was sweet beyond anything I could have expected, and it seemed that she felt it too. It was an unexpected response: music that was not at all romantic, but gave some sort of fierce pleasure, an eros of the mind, shared by us.

"You're mine…" I whispered at the end, and we both knew what I meant. For us the last song, "Sad-Eyed Lady of the Lowlands," was about her unhappy Southern California origins before I found her hitchhiking north to my Utah mountains, and all the dark

times since, her postpartum depression that took us to a brink
we thought we'd never retreat from, her tears with my arms
wrapped around her so she wouldn't hurt herself, and the
night I raced her to the medicine cabinet, grabbed the bottle of
Percocet before she could get it, ran outside and threw it with
all my might across the street into a weed-choked vacant lot.

She would sing along with passion, "█████ ██ █ █? █
█ █ █? █████ █████, ██ █████ ████," on
the chorus of "Like a Rolling Stone." That's a sentiment she
understood.

We found ourselves playing that album at low volume every
time we made love those months, which was more often than it
had been for many months before. We played it at other times
as well, quiet times, sitting together reading, or not-so-quiet
times, making dinner as Lily toddled around at our feet. *Blonde
on Blonde* meant us, together. Its lyrics became code, rich with
meaning that only we understood.

There were the obvious ones, like "I Want You." I might
whisper-sing an utterly unromantic couplet in her ear, "█
█ █████ ███, █████ █████ ████…"
and she'd smile and touch me as if to say "yes, later" because
she knew I was saying exactly what I didn't say, the chorus of
the song: "██ █, █ █, █████."

Later it became much more cryptic, like when we sat at the
dinner table with my parents, and without thought I emitted a
big sigh. My mom said, "Something bothering you, honey?" After
a beat I said, "Oh, nothing, just the guilty undertaker," and shot
a glance at Annie, who gave a little smile back. My mom said
"What?" and I shrugged but didn't have to respond as Annie broke
in, "Thank you for dinner, can I help clean up? We really should

get home," and her bare toes caressed my leg under the table, a promise. She wanted me, too.

Sometimes as we negotiated childcare or meal preparation, if one of us said or sang, "██ ████ ██ ██ ██ ..." it contained the unspoken next line, "████ ██ ██ ████, ██," and it meant something about good will, giving our time, a pledge to do whatever the other needed, for love. At one time or another, every one of the fourteen songs on the double album came up in our coded communications.

Our friends and family, small town Mormons, were mostly clueless about it and often must have thought we were nuts. Those days, we were living in a basement apartment below my mom and stepdad, paying low rent, getting childcare help from them whenever possible, saving money so I could go back to school. One day at a neighbor's backyard barbecue, a woman we barely knew was complaining at unbearable length about being laid off from her factory job, and Annie, without a hint of song or humor, quoted from "Rainy Day Women #12 & 35." "██, ████ ██ ██ ██ ██ ██ ██ ██ ██." And I chimed in, deadpan, with that repeated verb phrase that led to a rhyme. "██, ████ ██ ██ ██ ██ ██ '██ ██.'" And Annie said with exaggerated sincerity, the lead-in to the two-line chorus, "██ █ ██ ██ ██ ██ ██—" and then she spluttered into laughter. I tried to continue, "████ ██—" but I couldn't help myself, I joined in, an explosion of entirely inappropriate hilarity that left the woman gaping at us before she shook her head in disgust and walked away.

I saw my mother frowning and knew she had overheard...it was one more thing to cement her carefully hidden disapproval of Annie, the girl who had interrupted my good-Mormon-boy trajectory: college, mission, temple marriage, bishop-hood.

Annie was a high school dropout, a decision she had come to regret once she felt the chains of motherhood. She envied the meager two years of higher education that I had at that point. Our goal was that she would get back to school someday, after I had a degree. One Sunday morning over breakfast, she said, "You know I've been reading that Mark Twain book, right? *Letters from the Earth.* Satan writing letters back home to God about how crazy humans are, the silliness of politics, stuff like that. Well, I've been thinking about how he is such a uniquely American writer, and so is Bob Dylan. Like, each in his own time, a voice from the center of America. A critical voice, sometimes funny, sometimes not. Does that make sense?"

"Sure. Could make a good thesis for a college paper." I felt paternal, wanted to encourage anything intellectual, scholastic. But also, I liked her thoughts.

She continued, "And the feeling I get from both of them is sort of the same...I smile at the surprises, the ideas and clever phrases, the whadyacallit—the tone. They make me happy."

"Yeah, me too, I get it. It's like good-natured sarcasm. *A Connecticut Yankee in King Arthur's Court.* 'Leopard-Skin Pill-Box Hat'." Now I was totally with her on this. I did a loud, nasal Dylan impression of that song's funniest line: "███ ██ █ ██████ █ ███ ██ ████ █ ███ ██ █ ███ ██ ███."

"Yeah, so...what if...what if Bob Dylan was the reincarnation of Mark Twain?"

"Wow. Yeah, maybe it's true...ha! Little Bobby Zimmerman wonders why he has dreams about Huck Finn floating down the river. It's like the Dalai Lama, born again." I genuinely loved her idea, and I loved laughing with her. "We can teach that to our kids, piss off their school!"

We were so young then, just children raising children. The Dylan game, just like our infatuation, couldn't retain its life force in the face of everyday living. Pediatrician visits, babysitters, menial jobs for both of us, another pregnancy, pre-school, rent, car repairs.... The fun drained away, and soon the Dylan songs only came up in moments of anger and pain. Once she had wanted to be told that she made love "Just Like a Woman" but now she hated the suggestion that she would "███ ██ ██ █ ██ █." Our best thing had become our worst.

Annie never did go back to school, and her Twain-Dylan idea was never mentioned again. I felt her resentment of me. Then came my misguided attempt to launch us into proper middle-class life with a fancy job in New York, a fancy house in New Jersey. I wanted to give her what she wanted. But the roof beams of our marriage were silently falling on our heads as we pretended everything was fine—until a silly, minor conflict became the death knell. She had decided she wanted to plant a hedge along the edge of our yard, using Ceniza, also called Texas Sage. She loved the ashy-green shade of its leaves and the luscious pink flowers. I told her it was a desert plant; it would never survive our winters. We argued. Nowadays I regret the paternal, superior tone I took with her so often; it's ludicrous since I was only three years older. She planted the Ceniza. It died.

When I was self-righteously telling her "I told you so," she walked in silence to our turntable, pulled out the second disc of *Blonde on Blonde*, and put the needle down on track one: "Most Likely You Go Your Way and I'll Go Mine." Then she walked out of the room. I stood there and forced myself to listen.

From there everything seemed to tumble. I couldn't keep up with her twists of logic, her bizarre accusations. Our kids cried when we fought, which was often. And at the same time, my job in the city had become a form of torture as surreal as the lyrics of "Stuck Inside of Mobile with the Memphis Blues Again." Everything had to change. One night, late, we sat in misery at our dining room table. She was crying. I felt dumb. I didn't usually call her "mama," but it was heartfelt when I whispered the question, "██, ████, ██████?"

The answer was yes.

C.5 Two New Clues

A.J. STAYED UP LATE that Sunday night, reading and re-reading the half-dozen stories by Robbie Brand in the stack of little magazines. It was clear to see why Molly was upset and why she assumed he was the culprit: "Dylan Time" and "The Tunnel Diner" especially, written in first-person about intimate details in their early relationship.

The stories written in first person felt like the most insidious invasion of all. I *am I*, he thought. *You are not!*

All of it was a wrenching, disorienting walk through his life, but not precisely through his memories. There was something about the way language was used: word choice, sentence length, details emphasized, subtle inflections of tone, even point of view...for example, "The Seed" had an element of psychological awareness that he never experienced. There was another mind between his own and the page, like a window with tinted glass. Or, as he knew so well, like the way a cameraman and a video editor, despite the best intentions, turn real events into a distorted record that can never be fully trusted.

He was reading about himself and not-himself. He had become a fiction.

This even seemed true for "The Tunnel Diner," which he thought he recognized (how can foggy memory ever be sure?) as being almost exactly the words he had scribbled on a legal pad in the middle of that strange night five years ago. The pad that he lost. That he must have left at the motel. So maybe that was it—a clue to pursue! Maybe a door was finally opening. He would walk through it this week; that was the new plan.

The cumulative effect of his reading was that he had to give up on the dim idea that maybe Molly was Robbie Brand. Beside the fact that she had never shown the slightest interest or gift for writing, there were just too many details she couldn't have known. For instance, the story "Another War" was his alone, almost entirely beyond Molly's awareness, set in the years after their divorce, with one scene directly from his childhood memories. And "Venison" contained nothing *but* his childhood. Even if he had mentioned those memories to her, he would never have been so specific.

She didn't write the stuff, so she was a victim of this anonymous creep as well. A.J. regretted yelling at her earlier; she seemed to always bring out the worst in him.

Next, A.J. also spent an hour perusing his old journals but, except for "Desert Vacation," he found no direct correspondence between them and the stories. There were random overlaps here and there, but the journals were clearly not the source. It was as if the stories were pulled from the white spaces between the lines of his rambling scrawls. Or worse, as if a stranger lived in his mind.

That thought sent a current coursing up his spine and made the tiny hairs on his neck stand up. Was he doing this himself? Was he split? In the grip of Multiple Personality Disorder, a writer and photographer inhabiting one body, living two lives? Was he a sick, sick man?

But then, paging through his journals, he came across something else, something he'd entirely forgotten. It had an underlined heading: "Felicity and the Stranger." It was an account told to him by Felicity way back in the fall of 1989, just a few months after they met. She was still working at the Tunnel Diner then. An oddly-behaving customer had left behind a notebook that contained secrets about her life. It had disturbed her deeply, but then nothing had come of it.

The strangeness of her tale had struck A.J.'s fancy and he had written it out fully in the wee hours after she told him. He had imagined he would shoot photos of Felicity, the diner and its patrons, the gritty Jersey City scene, for some sort of hybrid story-and-image piece for publication—or maybe make a short film, if he could get funding. Another project that never saw fruition. This was in those limbo days pending his divorce when he lived in a drafty outbuilding on a Sussex County farm, planning his career change, dealing with lawyers, all such a blur now. He wondered, is it possible she still has that abandoned notebook? Could that customer have been Robbie Brand? Another trip to New Jersey was in order.

C.6 "Felicity and the Stranger," a Film Sketch by A.J. Campbell

Winter was approaching and the weather was nasty. Felicity was on the evening shift at the Tunnel Diner. A tall man with black-rimmed glasses sat at the counter, having dinner, as he often did. This was her sweetheart, Bo. The food was lousy, he had told her, but he didn't care. He wanted to be near her.

At table three was the young guy who she had hoped would not come back. He'd been in twice during the last couple of weeks, always in the mid-afternoon. He looked harmless enough, an average college kid who spoke politely when he ordered pie and coffee, but he gave her the willies. His eyes would follow her like a spotlight, then he'd bend his head and scribble like mad in a composition notebook, then he'd watch her again, then scribble again. When she would stop at his table to check in, refill his coffee, bring the check, he would quickly close the notebook and put on a fake smile, as if his obvious stalker behavior was invisible.

After the second time, she had told Bo about the guy. Not because she expected him to do anything about it; she just needed to vent. "Sounds like some preppie thinks he's a writer, out slummin' amongst the workin' class," Bo said in his slow Louisiana way.

Now the guy was here again. Felicity was not a confrontive person, but she *was* a Jersey girl. She was good-n-ready to give the kid a piece of her mind. In her peripheral vision, she saw his head swivel, following her as she carried two full plates to table nine, and then again as she went to the coffee station. Pot in hand, she leaned across the counter toward Bo and said in a low voice, "That writer guy is back. I'm gonna talk to him."

The kid's eyes were on his page as he wrote feverishly. He looked up, momentarily startled when she appeared at his table.

"Refill?" she said.

He slammed the notebook shut and put on a smile. "Oh, sure, thank you!"

She poured, then stood and stared at him. He smiled up at her. "Thank you," he said again.

"Look, buddy, we're glad for your business and all, but what's your problem?"

"Whadya mean?" His eyes glanced beyond her, then up at her face. He looked scared.

"I mean, why do you keep staring at me, then writing stuff? Let me see what you're writing." She held out her free hand for the notebook.

He grabbed it and stuffed it under his backpack on the bench seat next to him. That's when Bo showed up at her side.

The kid looked up at Bo, then at her. "I'm not doing anything wrong. It's a free country."

"Hey, son. That free country stuff only goes as far as when you start invadin' someone's privacy." Bo's voice was calm, even kind, but it was deep and no-nonsense.

Felicity's hand was still out. "Come on. Hand over the notebook."

"No, it's private property." He was sliding away from them on the seat.

Bo's voice got hard. "Well, this place is private property too, and you're not welcome here." He grabbed the kid's shoulder. The kid wriggled and shrugged.

"C'mon, buddy, just go." Felicity said. She put the coffee pot on the table, ready to get physical. The kid tried to knock Bo's hand away as he leaned further back, pulling Bo off balance. Bo yanked him hard.

"Hey!" the kid said. "Help!" Everyone in the diner was watching, silent.

In that instant the door swung open wide with a loud squeak and a gust of cold wind. In swept a small, gnarled figure, swathed and hooded in black, shoulders and head coated in sleet. An ancient woman's nut-brown face peered out, eyes wild. Her arthritic hands flailed about like birds as she shouted with an amazingly loud and gravelly voice: "Esta es la boca del diablo! Tunnel! Tunnel! Esta es boca del diablo! El diablo!" She marched toward Bo, shouting the same thing over and over.

Bo let go of the kid's shoulder to face the woman, his eyes gone wide.

"Maria!" Felicity said. "You can't come in here!"

The kid, suddenly free, grabbed his backpack and slithered past Bo, out the door. He speed-walked past the dripping windows and was gone.

"Maria, I'm sorry, but..." Felicity gently but firmly put her hands on the woman's shoulders and guided her, still shouting, toward the door. "You have to go home. You can't do this."

"Esta es boca del diablo!" was the last thing they heard as she went out into the storm.

Felicity faced the startled customers. "Sorry, everybody. That's happened before. She'll go home. She always does."

Bo still stood there, looking blank. He hadn't seen that sort of thing back in Baton Rouge.

"Thanks, babe," Felicity said to him. "Go finish your dinner." She picked up the coffee pot from the kid's table, and then she saw it: the notebook was still there, on the seat.

As she carried it behind the counter, she caught Bo's eye, waggled the notebook, and they both grinned. It went onto the shelf under the cash register as she rang out a young woman, and that's where it stayed until her shift was over. When Bo left, he told her in a low voice, "I know you're gonna read that thing tonight. I'll be waitin' to hear about it."

She did read it that night, and there were many times later when she wished she hadn't. It was an impressionistic, fragmented monologue full of outrageous blather and sarcasm that, unexpectedly, was not about her—except obliquely. It was entirely focused on her 12-year-old son, Bernard, purporting to be in his voice. In the voice of a mute boy.

It made no sense. Why had the kid been watching her? Clearly, he had quite an imagination to be able to create such a fantastic fiction. But the part that made her feel sick, invaded, afraid, was that there were secrets revealed. Her personal secrets. Things no one knew but her. She didn't even think Bernard knew, but this writer certainly did. How? How did he know? And now, how could she let Bo read it?

EVENTUALLY, SHE DID LET Bo read it. But she delayed for over a week, making excuses, shrugging it off as nothing, changing the subject when he asked about it. Partly, this was to give her time to question Bernard, to see if she could discern whether he'd been approached by that writer kid and somehow communicated things to him. Or whether something even worse had happened. Bernard shook his head no and no again, and wrote on his pad, *Don't know any such person. Haven't told anybody anything.*

Bo asked several times, but when she finally decided to share the notebook with him, it wasn't because of the pressure he put on her. It was because she came to a big, important realization: if their love was real, it could stand this test. She had to trust.

At his apartment after a delicious dinner of Crawfish Etouffee over rice, she slid the notebook across the table toward him. "I confess I've been hiding this from ya, babe. I'm sorry. It's a wild buncha silly nonsense, but it has my true secrets in it. I don't know how that creepy kid knew them, and that makes my stomach hurt just t'think about it. But they're in here, and there's no point in me pretendin' they're not true. You need to know." Bo blinked twice behind his glasses and nodded. She said, "I'll clean up and wash the dishes. You go sit on the couch and read."

Without a word, Bo took the notebook to the living room. When she finished the dishes, she sat next to him on the couch. The closed notebook was on his lap.

He took a deep breath and looked directly at her in his unruffled way. "Well. There's some sick shit in here, and I'd like to knock that little punk's block off."

Felicity felt worried until he put both her hands between his big rough ones. "But the parts about you, sweetie—those are not a problem at all. Hey, I wasn't born yesterday, I've made plenty of mistakes too. I mean, if there's even such a thing as mistakes—who the hell knows?"

Tears sprang to her eyes. "But...with a priest?"

"I know, part of you wants to hang on to guilt, but I'll say it again—it don't matter. The guy should be fired from his holy bullshit job, but that's none of my business. And the abortion was exactly what was called for in the situation."

She leaned her head on his chest, quietly crying, and he hugged her closer, kissing her hair.

It was soon after this that they began to speculate on what it might be like to live together. And—who knows?—even more. Maybe they could own a business. Like, how about a Cajun restaurant?

D. The Writer

D.1 What Is

Is THERE EVER A single decisive turning point? Or do huge changes in one's life take place in tiny increments, a gradual curve of the path? There can never be an answer; there is only what is.

Now a dark magician strides through the world with black cape billowing, people's lives tumbling in his wake.

D.2 Molly, the Fall, and Everything After

WHEN MOLLY CAMPBELL ANSWERED his knock on the door, Brandt said without hesitation the thing he had invented just seconds earlier: "Hello ma'am, I'm earning my way through college and I'm wondering if you would like me to mow and edge your lawn? Once every week or two, for the rest of the summer?" He

couldn't explain why he felt so irresistibly attracted to her, nor
where he got the skill to hide it.

Molly stared at him a beat, then she broke into that pretty smile
he learned about later, the one that says she's playing with you, cat
and mouse. "Well...hmm...I don't know. You think I need that?"

"Um, okay...let's not say need, let's say want. You *want* your yard
to look good."

"Yes, I do." She smiled at him for a long moment and he resisted
the urge to blab. Then she said, "Alright, then, it's a deal. What's
your name?"

This question he hadn't prepared for, but he was in top form
that day. "Brett," he said. "Brett Robinson." It was his third identity in two months. *What the hell, why not?*

Over the next few weeks, he was there every Saturday, did a good
job on the lawn, played a bit with the kids, and caught several
moments of eye contact with Molly that couldn't be denied. When
she asked him to start doing the yard work on Sundays when Lizzie
and Max were gone with their dad, Brandt knew exactly what was
going to happen.

It's very mysterious what physical intimacy can do. Until that
day, Brandt was aware that he was oddly bound to A.J. Campbell
in some way that seemed deeper than just stealing his scribbled
story, but he was entirely unprepared for the full consequence of
what came next.

He kissed A.J.'s wife. In a slant of afternoon window light, they
undressed each other. They pulled down clean blue sheets and
got into A.J.'s bed together. Brandt put his face in her hair and
breathed deeply, the same breath A.J. must have taken. Brandt
caressed her skin as A.J. had done, felt in his hands the weight of
her breasts, precisely the same feeling A.J.'s hands had known. The

warmth between her thighs, he shared with A.J. As he entered her, a slow exquisite inch at a time, Brandt knew he was changing. In this very moment, he was becoming more and more that other man, less and less himself. She sighed and moaned, cheeks flushed pink, eyes closed. He breathed slow and deep to hold back, a sudden unknown phrase in his mind: *the ghost of electricity howled in the bones of her face.* They moved together. With every passing second, a door opened wider to some sort of universal place where there were no divisions, where everyone's story belonged to everyone else. Surely A.J. was there too, so close, a breathy gibberish in his ear. Or was it himself whispering? No, no self was there, only the whispers. Whispers or merely ragged inhales, exhales, lips on skin, boundaries lost, flooded with shreds of unfamiliar thought, flickering images like confetti, scraps of conversation, foreign memories, a stormy wave of churning emotion that he could barely ride until they reached a breathless, sweaty end.

This was something utterly new. Not love; not anything with a name. She had blasted out his insides, drilled a gaping channel open to the sky, the empty night sky with all its tiny, cold, glittering voices. His life could never be the same again.

Now, so many years later, Brandt sits at a desk and stares into space. Every time he looks back on that summer afternoon, it's with a twisted mix of gratitude and regret. His life's course was set, his livelihood, his glory. His doom.

From that day forward, he has held this secret: he is a man outside of science, a supernatural freak. No one else, except maybe the insane, can do what he can do. He has a pure, direct access to some realm of mysterious energy, a vast invisible cloud buzzing with thoughts and memories and emotions of random people everywhere. He is a human antenna, with almost zero control over what he receives. At any moment, a channel may open and he'll need to be ready to take dictation: poise fingers on keys, listen, type like a madman, collapse. In the beginning it was all about A.J.—his childhood, youth, marriage, career, hopes and dreams and pain—but gradually other people began to filter in, whispers that soon grew to a roar.

Early on, he had to rethink his arrogant reaction to A.J.'s story about the homeless weirdo, Ashton Gill, who heard the sounds of the universe. Brandt had dismissed it to himself: *Well, that's some crazy lunatic shit, but I'll use it anyway.* Now he can't deny his own experience.

His relationship with Molly couldn't last, of course. *We're so in love*, Brandt had thought at first. Naturally; what kid wouldn't? But his naiveté soon became clear, and by early fall it was over. As the weeks went by, she grew strangely coy, then cold. She never showed any interest in Brandt's life, so when he got the letter telling him he had won the story contest his professor had asked him to enter, he didn't mention it to her.

There was a Sunday in late August when it seemed, even though Brandt could hardly believe it, that Molly tried to get them caught by A.J., who was returning the kids from visitation. As he was dressing, Brandt overheard her on the phone saying, "Sure, come back early if you need to." But she didn't say anything to him; in fact, she tried to lure him back into bed. Feeling uneasy, he rushed to load his gear into the truck and was just pulling away from the curb as A.J. drove into the driveway. Brandt's heart was pounding, but he nodded with macho nonchalance at this central character who loomed in his life, this man he was seeing for the first time. And to whom he was nobody.

It was a couple of weeks later, over a pleasant post-coitus snack of grapes and cheese, that Molly looked up and said, "Just so you know...I've been faking my orgasms. The whole time." He stared at her, stunned, silent. Her eyes on his, she bit a grape in two, with a smile that showed her teeth.

It hurt, of course, a bruise that lingered, but the worst part was that he couldn't tell: was she lying or not? Truth would be bad; lying would be worse. This was some type of perverse malice that Brandt couldn't understand. But of course, he was a liar as well. What could he say?

The sex between them had grown gradually dull; never again was there anything like that first time. In October, he said, "I doubt your lawn will need any more mowing this season." She agreed, and he knew what it meant.

Still, so many little things stick in his memory: the dance her fingertips would always do, drumming a surface while she awaited her turn to speak. The way she flipped her hair with a cute grin and a "Just kidding!" but too late, the cut was made. The candy bribes and "consequence" threats to get her children to behave. And he hated seeing the torn photo hanging on the refrigerator: Molly and the smiling kids, with A.J. obviously ripped away. He wondered why she would let it stay there for Lizzie and Max to see, every day.

In the end he was relieved to leave that house behind.

Nowadays he can see that she was just another sad young woman, looking for love then pushing it away, bringing wounds from infancy and childhood along with her, unacknowledged. Like him, like everyone.

Autumn descended, and he was alone again, more alone than ever. From that fall, 1989, he remembers three things. First, the Berlin Wall came down. The end of the Cold War, the dawn of a new era, all the professors said. Brandt's generation had a rosy future, free from fear! For him it was something different: the two halves of a split city now facing each other like two halves of a single person, staring into a mirror, attracted, afraid, wondering how to merge.

Second, "The Tunnel Diner" appeared in print in the student magazine *Pratfall*. The story looked alien on the page, in its formal dress, typeset and permanent, and it made Brandt wonder: *Who am I? Who am I in relation to this, this genuine artifact of Twentieth Century Literature?* But he received much praise around school, so he didn't ponder long. On his new path through life, the wet cement was beginning to harden.

Third, he began to venture deeper in, further out. Some dark magnet was pulling him, an irresistible force. He found himself in Jersey City, in the actual Tunnel Diner, on two sunny afternoons and then on a bitter cold night with sleet scratching the windows, watching a waitress whose name was...yes, Felicity.

Felicity and her silent son, he who would not speak except in text beaming in through Brandt's open channel, tuning in most clearly there at the grand entrance to the underground. "This is the mouth of the devil!" cried the scary old crone from the dirty streets. So true.

After the tall man with glasses ejected Brandt from the diner, a girl followed him out, catching up to him before he reached his car, two blocks away.

"They shouldn't have done that to you," she said. She was about Brandt's age, pretty, with somber brown eyes and wavy dark hair under the jacket hood she had raised against the ice falling from the sky.

"Yeah," Brandt said, his shoulders hunched. "Get in, we'll talk about it." He unlocked the passenger door and was surprised when she climbed in without hesitation.

"Drive me to my hotel?" she asked. It was only a few blocks away. She had hitchhiked from Utah in search of her lost brother Danny, and had not yet entered New York City—hesitating, perched on the cusp you might say, looking for a sign. She invited him to her room, no sex, she was a Mormon girl, and they talked about many, many things, like foreigners learning each other's foreign ways. They fell asleep side by side under the covers.

In the heart of the night with the 24-hour tunnel traffic humming, Brandt thinks he awakes to find himself naked and the girl naked on top of him, full body, skin to skin, and they move together with whispers, caresses, lips and flesh and hair, and she is murmuring close in his ear...that they've met before, long before, in the diner, the Tunnel Diner, and he doesn't understand but doesn't care...and it's all about merging, a slow blur of urgent, half-seen, fully-felt communion, fingertips, lips, skin, immersion, until a mutual end from which he slips back into dreams that perhaps he had never left at all.

When morning light woke him, Brandt was alone. He found a note. "Thank you B. You were just what I needed. May we meet again...Jill Ashe."

That name...so close, so close, to the man in A.J.'s story. Ashton Gill, the phantom. Some kind of message was here, but what was it? Everything was foggy, but even fog makes patterns sometimes, foggy patterns, a fuzzy code. Brandt could not decipher this code, and so he gave up, and moved on.

So Felicity and Bernard joined into the transmission, that first fall. Thus began another chapter, and on and on they went, chapter after chapter, mind after mind, in all the years after...too many, too many to tell.

Winter came, and the world tipped over into a new decade, the century's last. The new mask Brandt wore, the "writer" persona, carried him through the rest of college, out of the motel job and away from his proud father's carpet business, into New York City. He imagined his mother's voice: "What an amazing gift you've been given. Don't waste it!" Molly Campbell had already begun to recede into his past, even as she stayed ever-present in the stories, A.J.'s stories, that filled Brandt's head to bursting, day in, day out...for a couple more years, until they too faded away, drowned out by other voices.

Now, a man alone for years and years, he looks at the books on his shelves, the books with his name on them. Each of his various names, all the names that don't describe him.

He takes a deep breath, fills his lungs, holds it, lets it out. Slowly, slowly.

Done.

D.3 What Is Not

There is no truth here; everything in this book is a lie.

Consider the statement above. Is it true? If so, it is also false. If it's false, it's true. I am a logician's contradiction.

Must the statement be either true or false? Perhaps it is neither. Perhaps it is both; that would be my preference. The concept is called Dialetheism: the proposition that the liar paradox is *both* true and false. Is it possible? Imagine...holding the thing and its opposite always in your hand, without conflict, with only acceptance.

Such a thing is purely imaginary, like the square root of negative one. It does not exist in what we call "the real world." Mathematicians posit the "imaginary number" i, defined solely by the property that its square is negative one: $i^2 = -1$. Algebra then shows that both i and $-i$ are square roots of negative one. They are opposites, yet equal.

"I" as in the ego, as in first-person narration, as in the storyteller himself.

Both I and not-I, self and not-self, the idea and its own negation, the existing body and the empty space of its non-existence.... Together as one, they hover in imaginary space, equals and opposites, eternally.

D.4 "Venison," a Short Story by Robbie Brand

EVERY FALL WHEN I was a child, a dead deer hung by its antlers from a tree branch in our yard. Through a long slit up its belly I glimpsed an empty red cavity. I watched with fascination as my silent father made several careful cuts through the hide, starting around the neck, then peeled the skin down bit by bit, gently slicing the translucent connecting tissue, pulling the skin, slicing again, pulling again, until the gray-brown hide lay in a heap on the ground and the deer was naked, skinny and pink.

Throughout the winter and spring, we selected various-shaped, white-paper packages from the freezer, or we opened home-canned jars of brown meat from the pantry shelves, and gathered potatoes, carrots, turnips, and onions from our chilly root cellar, so that our five-member family could feast on hearty roasts and stews. My mother would tell us how grateful we should be, and we thanked Heavenly Father at every meal. It wasn't until I was nearly an adult and had become aware of the everyday gluttony of America that I realized how meager our table really was.

Besides running our small farm and sheep business, my dad was a hunter, from a hunting family. Deer, elk, pheasant, turkey. As a young child, I was only allowed on his fishing trips, and I loved them best on those rare occasions when he took only me and left my mother and sisters behind. But I was waiting for the day I would get access to that exclusive world of men, men without women, men with guns tracking beasts of prey in the wilderness. Finally, I turned ten and the door was opened.

That's when the conflict began. Sunday was the preferred hunting day for my dad and his three younger brothers, even though they were Mormons born and raised, just like me. But for my mother, Sunday was the Sabbath—a day for worship only, hunting season or not. I had been dimly aware of the occasional tension between them but there must have been a truce of sorts—until that Saturday when my dad declared he was taking me hunting with him. We would leave at dawn the next morning.

"No! Jimmy needs to go to church," she said.

"He gets plenty of church all year. He's going with me." My dad always spoke quietly and firmly.

"But he's only two years away from being ordained to the priesthood. He shouldn't miss *any* spiritual teachings now!"

"He'll be fine. I'm fine. Me and my brothers are all fine—we got ordained, we go to church, but we also go hunting."

"You're *fine*? You go to church? You almost never go! You've abandoned it. I won't let Jimmy follow you down that path!" The shrill edge of her voice made me cringe. But then it got worse. She turned to me.

"Jimmy, I know you love the gospel, you're learning it so well, and you're a special spirit. You'll be such a good deacon. Please keep the Sabbath holy." Her begging was like a weight on my chest.

"Meredith, don't put him in the middle," my dad said.

They were both looking at me. I was finding it hard to breathe. But I managed to say, "I...I want to go hunting."

Tears filled her eyes and she turned away, shaking her head, a mixture of sadness and disgust on her face. I felt both guilty and elated. I looked at my dad and he nodded, no smile, no words.

During those few weeks of hunting season this scene was repeated several times, with variations that included references to my eternal salvation and my holy callings, and to his failures as a family patriarch, as a spiritual leader, as a man. She never gave up, but he held firm. My feelings were all jumbled—I loved my mom, I knew she was a sweet and kind person; I remembered her reading bedtime stories to me, tickling me into a laughing fit, putting a cool rag on my forehead when I was feverish. But I went with my dad on every hunting trip that year.

The first one was unusual because he wasn't hunting, he was just accompanying his brother. It was bow season, and my dad was considering whether to become a bow hunter. His boisterous youngest brother, Uncle Jack, had purchased a bow that I found beautiful—its variegated shades of inlaid wood with a glossy finish, its perfect curve that went from straight to arched as Jack bent it and attached the heavy bowstring. And its power. I didn't have the strength to draw it at all. This was a strong man's weapon. Besides the bow itself, I loved the long, straight, yellow arrows, the striped gray feathers of their fletching, and most of all the perfect symmetry of the murderous, razor-sharp arrowheads.

Uncle Jack arrived before sunrise in his Mustang. He said the thing he always said, ever since he'd learned of my love for the King Arthur stories: "Greetings, Sir James!" I liked him. We loaded into Dad's ancient pickup, me in the middle of the bench seat and two rifles on the rack behind our heads. Our first stop was the all-night café near the interstate, where we sat at the counter for bacon and eggs, two coffees and a hot chocolate. Coffee is a sin, but it's what men drink. I was thrilled and knew I could never tell my mother.

After breakfast we drove an hour east of our central Utah town, with Uncle Jack whistling country hits because there was no radio in Dad's truck. On the high plateau above Fish Lake, we parked on an isolated dirt road and began walking single file, diagonally uphill through sagebrush and junipers. Jack went first, carrying his strung bow, a quiver of arrows on his back, followed by my dad. I came last, determined to keep up. Almost no words were spoken; for nearly an hour I heard only the music of our boots crunching on sand and stones. We had just entered a crowded grove of skinny pines when Jack stopped and gave a loud whisper: "Norman! Buck at eleven o'clock!"

My dad and I froze and looked where he pointed. I saw a gray-brown shape barely moving, the exact color of the tree trunks.

Its head was lowered, grazing. I couldn't see any antlers. Jack was immediately down on one knee, fitting an arrow to the string, then left arm out straight, right hand slowly pulling back to his cheek. He held it for just a breath, then let it go. I heard a faint swish, a thwack, and I saw the deer jump straight up, its back hunched, the arrow jutting from its shoulder. I caught just a glimpse of its small antlers before it was gone, bounding away into the thick stand of trees.

"I got 'im, Norman, I got 'im!" Jack's eyes were wide.

"You sure did." My dad's voice was calm. "Now we gotta follow 'im and hope he don't get far."

For the next two hours we tracked the deer, following spots of blood on the ground, broken branches, hoof prints. It was slow, tedious guesswork...to me it seemed hopeless. Then Jack stopped, bent to the ground, and turned to us with dismay on his face. He held an eighteen-inch length of arrow shaft stained with six inches of blood. It meant that the steel head and ten inches of shaft were still embedded in the deer, wherever it was.

"Damn, Jack, this is not good," my dad said. "We're never gonna find 'im, and he's just gonna die out here somewhere."

I had never seen fun-loving Uncle Jack look unhappy. Now he was a glum stranger. "Shit!" he said and sat heavily on the ground. Dad and I sat too. We shared water and beef jerky, then headed back to the truck.

No more than ten minutes down the road, Jack said, "Slow down! Deer!" He was pointing into a patch of bigger pines on our right. My dad slowed and stopped, and we got out silently, again following Jack into the woods, trying to tread as quietly as possible. *Like Indians*, I thought.

I glimpsed a buck with two does, moving leisurely through the underbrush uphill from us. They stopped to graze, and the scene repeated itself: Jack drew back his arrow, let it fly, and all three deer bolted, disappearing as if they had never been there.

Jack was suddenly excited again. "I swear I got 'im!" We clambered as quickly as we could to where the deer had been, and there on the slope behind where the buck had stood, an arrow was stuck in the ground. Jack sighed, "Ugh, guess I missed."

"Nope." My dad picked up the arrow, which was intact this time—but its full length was covered with green slime tinged with blood. "It went right through his gut. That deer's a goner."

"Oh, no..." Jack groaned.

My dad's face had never looked more stormy. There was a darkness in his scowl that scared me. His voice was flat. "Jimmy, I want you to know: this is really bad. This is not what hunting is all about. It's not a damned *sport*. Now we've injured two deer who will suffer many hours until they die, and this will benefit no one but the buzzards. What we've done is just plain wrong, and I have learned this: I will never hunt with a goddam bow. We're going home now." That was the most words I had ever heard him say at one time.

All three of us were silent all the way home. I heard later that Uncle Jack had sold his archery gear to a friend. When rifle season for both deer and elk started the following month, everything was back to normal. We didn't speak of that day again.

But unexpected new thoughts had begun to arise in my ten-year-old mind. Without any real self-awareness, I was experiencing the beginnings of something akin to skepticism. Over the next weeks, I went on more hunting trips with Dad and Jack or his other brothers. I carried food and water, I kept up with them on the hikes, I felt a part of the society of men. I loved the mountain vistas, the rushing streams and dappled glades, the sunrises and sunsets. But I didn't love the sound of gunshots. I didn't love the sight of animals dashing in terror.

No one was having any luck until one frigid weekend in late October. Dad and Jack and I got out of the truck in the gray dawn light and stood in a row—big, little, big—to pee before we started hiking. Jack said, "Ah, the curse of the North: two inches of shriveled penis, four inches of clothes." My dad smiled and grunted something like a laugh. I couldn't help myself, I burst into giggles and almost peed on my boots.

As I walked behind them up a heavily wooded ridge, my nose began to run. I sniffed. A minute later I sniffed again. Then again and again. My dad stopped and turned around. "Jimmy, for god's sake, blow your nose."

"I don't have a tissue or a handkerchief."

"Do it like this." He closed one of his nostrils with a finger and blew snot out onto the ground.

"Really?"

"Do it."

I tried it and blew snot onto my own hand. I flicked it in disgust and wiped it on my pants.

"Other side too."

I did it again with the same embarrassing results. He shook his head and turned away, and we continued walking. My eyes stayed on the ground. I was surprised to find myself wishing I was at home in my room with my books, sketchpad, pencils.

The day was gloomy and cold. We walked and walked. At last, my dad spotted a buck across a gully amongst many large old pines. I thought it looked majestic when it raised its antlered head. Dad leaned his left shoulder against a tree, the thirty-ought-six raised to his right shoulder, his eye to the scope.

The crack echoed in the canyon and the deer dropped straight to the ground. We fought our way through undergrowth, down one slope and up the other. The buck was a good sized three-point, lying still as stone, legs twisted, eyes blind, tongue lolling out. Where had the majesty gone?

"Damn good shot, straight through the heart!" Jack said.

I watched as Jack held the deer's legs apart and Dad gutted it, slitting the white belly from anus to sternum, reaching in to cut the windpipe, and dragging out a purple mass of entrails that looked impossibly big. The guts slithered in one heap a few feet down the rocky slope and lay there steaming. Dad poured water from our canteen over his bloody hands, then wiped them on his jeans.

Jack used his hatchet to cut and trim a sapling, fashioning a long straight pole over which they tied the deer's hooves. They hoisted the pole to their shoulders, Dad at the head, Jack behind. I carried the food, water, and both rifles.

Then came the worst part of the day. A gutted male mule deer weighs close to two hundred pounds. The load on my skinny shoulders was about twenty pounds. There was no trail for us to follow. It was step by torturous step, down into the rocky, overgrown ravine and back up the other side, footings treacherous on leaves and gravel, struggling over fallen trees, clothing and antlers snagged by twigs, the deer's back often scraping against the ground. Dad and Jack would need to stop every few minutes to catch their breath, or to gather strength for a herculean lift of their burden over a log or boulder. Their faces were beaded with sweat despite the cold. I was overheated under my coat but my fingers were numb, and my legs began to feel shaky. The rifle stocks banged my thighs, the barrels catching on branches. It must have taken over an hour just to get back to the primitive little trail that ran along the ridge where we'd been walking when we spied the buck.

We rested, drank, snacked, then resumed our journey. It was a little easier now, fewer obstacles, but still the trail went uphill and down. Unburdened, we could have reached the truck in an hour. But we were already exhausted. My dad looked pale and grim. We trudged in silence except for harsh breathing and an occasional groan, with periodic stops to shift the load. My shoulders hurt. I was in a mindless trance, putting one foot in front of the other, and I knew they were suffering even more. I have no idea how long it took, but finally we reached the road.

Dad and Jack rested the deer on the ground before the final big lift into the truck. My dad's face scared me. It was even more pale than before, his eyes sunken in dark circles, his upper lip quivering. I had never seen his hands shake like this before. They both took deep breaths, counted to three, and heaved the deer up and into the empty bed of the pickup. The dull thud seemed like finality, a judge's gavel.

Immediately my dad fell like a tree to the ground. His breathing was deep and ragged, his eyes closed.

"Norman, Norman!" Jack moved to his side, knelt, lifted and cradled his head and shoulders. I was frozen, staring.

After three terrible seconds, my dad's eyes opened. "I'm okay," he said in a strained whisper. "Just hafta breathe." They stayed in that position for several long minutes as my dad's gasping slowed and calmed. Finally, he said, "Shit, that was not fun. Let's go."

Jack whooped. "Hooee! Thought you were gonna kick the bucket, old man. I'm driving." Together, we helped Dad to his feet and into the passenger seat. He slept on the way home, while I couldn't stop thinking about what I'd just seen. My dad had almost died. For what?

At the age of ten I could not have found the words, but I knew in some deep part of me that this day was a turning point. I had already betrayed my mother's dreams for me, and I somehow knew I would continue to do so. But now, I could see that I would betray my father as well. He was a good man, but I would never be like him. I could not be the son he hoped for, the adult son who would work beside him, shearing sheep, milking cows, butchering chickens, tilling gardens, hunting meat. That was not me. I could only be the man that my heart led me to be.

At home, under the darkening gray sky, my mother and sisters and I all watched as Dad and Uncle Jack used a block and tackle to hoist the dead buck out of the pickup and leave it dangling from the usual tree limb, to be skinned tomorrow. My mother was smiling, but I could see the hint of tension in her lips. She was not as good at covering her feelings as she thought she was. Would she ever approve of my dad again? Of me? I only knew that during the coming months, as we gathered at the table for venison and vegetables, she would lead the thankful prayers, and I, along with all my family, would bow my head and say, "Amen."

E. The Photographer

E.1 Long Jersey Monday

MONDAY MORNING WAS BLESSEDLY cool, with no work on
A.J.'s calendar—also a blessing, but a mixed one. His week
would get busy starting Wednesday morning, on a gig with
I.I.I. A.J. called ahead to make sure Felicity would be home,
then he strolled uptown and picked up the handsome 11x14
print, pre-mounted on foam core, that he'd ordered for her
birthday. He stopped at the nearby Sam Flax store and bought
a frame. He stood in the store and assembled the gift, slipped
it back into the bag without gift-wrapping, and set off for the
PATH train to Hoboken.

Felicity lived with her mother and son, plus the recently added
presence of her husband Bo, in a cramped single-family on a
crowded block where parking was impossible, away from the
trendy hotspots of Washington Street. Bo was a construction
worker from the South, a big guy who frowned at A.J. the first

time they met and said almost nothing, until an hour had passed and he apparently realized A.J. was not a threat.

Felicity's mother, wearing a gray bun and a shapeless housedress, opened the door at A.J.'s knock, gave him a sour look, and shuffled out of the room without a word. He smiled, knowing it was nothing personal; it was just who she was.

"Ohmigod!" Felicity squealed when she pulled the framed photo from the bag. "It's beautiful!"

"Look closer...who's that guy?" A.J. said. They sat side by side on the sofa.

She leaned forward, her face obscured by a wild mass of brass-colored hair, studied the image for several long seconds, then spoke softly. "No way...izzat really him?"

"I guess I can't be sure, but it really looks like him. Don't you think?"

"Well, my memory's not so good of that night. If you think it's him, it prob'ly is." Her brow wrinkled. "But wait, didn't you see the guy and talk to 'im when you took the picture?"

"No, it's weird—I just didn't notice him. Or, maybe it's not that weird. I had my eye on the camera and my watch...y'know, not on the individual faces. But still, look—it almost seems like *he* recognized *me*."

"Yeah. But he didn't say anything."

A.J. shrugged. "So maybe he doesn't want to be found. But if *this* can happen, maybe I can run into him again, by pure chance. Stranger things have happened in the big city."

She bent toward the photo again. "And look, is that a little kid with 'im? Maybe he lives in your neighborhood."

"That's what I'm counting on. By the way, I thought you were homeschooling Bernard. Where is he?"

"Bo's off today, so he took 'im out for a pizza lunch. Still working on making a connection, y'know?" She sighed.

"Tough situation. I'll see if I can get my kids over here one of these days."

"That would be great."

A.J. stood up and started pacing. "Okay, so now there's something else I need to talk to you about."

"Uh-oh, that sounds bad."

"No, it's not, but it means dredging up old memories. Five years ago, some guy left a notebook in the diner." He could tell by her face that she remembered instantly. "Do you still have it?"

She looked worried. "Why? What does it mean?"

"Well...something similar is happening to me. Right now. Some guy is writing stories about my life. Maybe it's the same guy."

"Oh, no. Tell me more. I know how upsetting that can be."

Not wanting to dwell on the emotional side of it, he told her quickly what had happened since he found the first story. She nodded and listened, ever the empath. But right now, he needed information. "I'm in suspense here. The notebook, do you have it?"

She shook her head. "I'm really sorry, A.J.. Me'n Bo burned the damn thing, a long time ago. Page by page, like a ceremony. Just wanted to be rid of it, y'know? It fucked up my mind."

"Shit. Okay." A.J.'s hopes lurched down, a sudden flat tire. He nodded as he paced. "I understand. Makes sense. So...can you tell me anything about the guy?"

"He was young, y'know, a kid. College or high school. Not the usual bum. That's what was weird. Dark hair, cleancut."

"Would you recognize him today?"

"Hmm, maybe, but I doubt it. He was sort of...generic, I guess."

A.J. stopped pacing. "It's a bummer. Dead ends everywhere I turn. I guess I should go now. Gotta drive out to the country today to chase another clue."

"Wait—maybe this will help. On the inside cover of the notebook, he had made a sort of doodle." She stood and moved across the room, picked up a pen and small pad from next to the phone, and began drawing. "It looked like this."

She showed A.J. the pad. Inside a square were two Rs and two Bs, stacked.

"Robbie Brand!" he almost shouted. "It's him—those are the author's initials!"

"Okay, that accounts for R.B. So maybe his real name is the opposite: B.R."

"Yes! Thank you, Felicity. This is great." He tore off the page and stuffed it in a pocket. "I gotta go now. Happy birthday again!" He hugged her and air-kissed her cheeks as she smiled. He set off through the backstreets of Hoboken, striding past faux-brick facades, pickup trucks, and bathtub Madonnas, then through the blocks where nannies strolled carriages past BMWs, and with perfect timing, caught the next train.

THE RIDE FROM HOBOKEN to Christopher Street, the first stop, is only eight minutes. Eight minutes to travel under one of the world's greatest rivers to one of the world's greatest cities, and into Greenwich Village, the village inside a city, where impossible things occur like the intersection of parallels: West 4th Street meets

West 10th Street, and more. The corner of West 4th and Jones Street, half a block from A.J.'s apartment, is where the iconic cover image of the album *The Freewheelin' Bob Dylan* was taken in 1963—the photograph that, according to Janet Maslin, "inspired countless young men to hunch their shoulders, look distant, and let the girl do the clinging."

A.J. had devoured his neighborhood's history, recent and non-, ingested it like nourishment, let it feed his every stride through the jumble of streets. He loved the place. That was one reason he didn't really want to drive to the outer fringe of New Jersey on this beautiful afternoon. But a dark specter was pushing him, an irrational rage.

He puttered about in his apartment for an hour, then took the annoying long walk down to the lot where he'd been forced to park after returning from his Jersey visitation the evening before. He had cruised his neighborhood first, spied a spot, and lost it to the car in front of him. The lot was always his last resort; it was relatively cheap and usually had space, trapped as it was in a hidden tangle between the Holland Tunnel entrance and the West Side Highway. Today, the whole thing made him angry.

Even though he was ahead of the torturous rush-hour crawl, it was still slow going to get out of the lot, then thread a circular maze of one-way streets east until he could merge with traffic approaching the tunnel, and finally get on his way west. His hands were fists on the wheel.

As he drove, he indulged his imagination, conjuring up a scene with multiple satisfying variations: at the motel, the sympathetic manager would give him the name and address of a creepy guy who had worked there five years ago, a name with the initials R.B. or B.R. No one had liked him; he was fired for theft. A.J. would drive to the creep's dumpy trailer, kick in the door, and confront him with his nasty crimes, bellowing in righteous fury. The slimy creep would confess and whine and beg for mercy, but A.J. had none, none whatsoever. He would pound the guy's face with his fist, to a bloody pulp. Or better yet, break all his fingers with a hammer so he could never write again. And *then* pound his face. What the hell, maybe he would use the hammer on the asshole's head, a full arm swing, whack whack whack whack!, completely fucking murder him. Let his body rot, no loss to anybody. That would take care of the problem once and for all, goddammit.

A.J.'s jaw was clenched and his shoulders stiff. His muscles felt like concrete. He was tired of driving.

The shadows were growing long as he found himself again in the territory of green farmlands, wooly hills, lakes, and housing tracts, out there in the pretty country, where most of his memories were painful. He remembered the streets of Lake Hopatcong in increments as he negotiated each curve, until there it was. Exactly what he never would have expected: the Marina Vista Motel was shuttered, with peeling paint, weeds in the parking lot, and a Sheriff's Office notice in the window.

A.J.'s forehead dropped to the steering wheel. Parked at the curb, he sat bent in despair for several long minutes as his unexpressed fury got stuffed down like laundry into a bag. Then he drove to the nearest bar.

The place was a shadowy dive: neon glinted across dark wood and a worn-out jukebox. During his first beer, he asked the bartender: "Who owns the Marina Vista Motel?"

"Hell if I know," she said.

During his second beer, he spoke to everybody sitting near him, loudly: "Anybody know who owns the Marina Vista Motel?"

Most of them shrugged, shook their heads. One guy said, "Go ask at the Town Offices. They open at nine in the morning."

During his third beer, he was silent. Then he stood up. "Fuck that," he muttered to no one.

He made it home in a liquid blur, unscathed, moving very carefully. Then, fitfully, he slept.

E.2 Terrible Tuesday

Waking was like a slow trudge from cell to gas chamber: the dreams were bad, the day would be worse. A.J. lay as if paralyzed, in timeless twilight. No light reached his bed. When he finally forced himself up, it was almost noon. He went through the rote motions of brewing coffee. The caffeine started up his mental gears, slowly, slowly. With his second cup came a phantasmagoric stew of scenes from his earlier life, but seen from strange angles, as if not his own view, as if he were remembering a movie, not his true story. Something felt shaky under his psychic feet; he was not standing on solid earth. He had the odd sense that he didn't even know his own name. The part of him that was able to observe all this then began to berate him for his weakness.

He was a sick, sick man, his skull inhabited by a malicious stranger.

For a crazy moment, he was tempted to dump all the literary magazines with the Brand stories into his kitchen sink and burn them. But that would only create more problems, both with his neighbors and with Molly.

The afternoon passed. He did nothing: read a week-old newspaper, read an article in an old Atlantic Monthly about a vacationing family who died in the Sahara.

The dark cloud wouldn't lift. By the time the sun had set, he couldn't stand the four walls any longer, and fled to the street. There at least was the distraction of faces, color, motion, voices, the never-ending visual and aural cacophony of the city.

An hour later, he found himself on Canal Street, but the crowds brought back his anger. He turned up Mercer Street, thankful for quiet. Then something woke up in his head: a memory of having walked this Soho block some years back. The streetlights glinting on cobblestones, the old buildings once bustling with industry, the fire escapes and dumpsters and graffiti and collages of posted flyers, the lightless windows, the absence of pedestrians...it could have been any block in Soho, where hidden gems might be found, off the bright bustle of Spring. But now he was getting a distinct vibration of recall. Yes, there it was: the empty storefront that once had housed the Museum of Holography. He had stumbled upon it in his early explorations of the city and been fascinated by all that was hidden behind its obscure facade: the three-dimensional images hanging in mid-air, the displays of holography's history and applications; the explanation of the laser science of holograms. And, of course, their fractal nature: how any piece of a hologram contains all the information of the entire hologram. He had bought a book there, *The Holographic Universe* by Michael Talbot, that was now sitting on a shelf in his apartment. The book was highly speculative but, whether scientifically valid or not, it had energized his imagination.

He stood now, staring at the dim outline of his reflection in the dark window, remembering passages in the book. The respected physicist David Bohm had theorized about the unseen truths of the universe. In what he called the "implicate order," the deepest level of reality, there is wholeness. The implicate order unfolds to display the "explicate order," which is the fractured reality we live in. This folding in and out takes place in a vast, constant pulsing...and so the realities are concurrent, the one we see and the one we don't see. It suggests a solution to the mystery of "quantum entanglement." Rather than causality or faster-than-light communication to explain the link between separated particles, the answer is in the implicate order. Bohm imagined a fish in a tank, with one video camera pointed at one side of the tank and another pointed at another side of the tank, at right angles to the first. The video screens for these cameras are in a different room. An observer of the two screens has no knowledge of the fish or the cameras. The two images are significantly different, apparently showing separate, unrelated objects, yet a connection is observed in their simultaneous movements. On that level of reality (analogous to our 3D world, the explicate order), the observer (us) might contrive various explanations of how the two objects are communicating with one another, or are "entangled." But at a deeper dimension of reality, we understand that there is only one fish, not two. No separation exists.

A.J. turned from the shadowy mirror and walked again, pondering ideas just outside his understanding. He knew it was an attempt to rise out of his sullen gloom, to forget Brand and Molly and the seismic fault in the ground of his own self. But it wasn't working. His shoulders were still hunched, his steps heavy.

Gradually his thoughts shifted to Paul Auster's novella *City of Glass*, in which a detective mapped out the footsteps of a man he was surveilling, a language specialist whose sanity was in question, who seemed to just be wandering aimlessly around the Upper West Side. But when plotted on paper, the man's rambling route spelled the letters of a message: "The Tower of Babel." *What does* my *wandering say?* A.J. wondered.

Later, he didn't know what time, he found himself heading east on St. Marks Place, leaving the congestion between 2nd and 3rd Avenues behind. He was thirsty and his feet were tired. On the sidewalk was an A-frame chalkboard in front of a little bar called Sin-é. The windows were plastered with posters of someone A.J. didn't know, Jeff Buckley, and scrawled on the sign under *Tonight* was another name he didn't recognize, Eric Wood.

He went in. The place was dim but not dark; pale textured walls seemed to jut at odd angles. There was a scattering of people at tables and a dark-haired man was tuning his guitar in the tiny space apparently meant as the stage, demarcated only by two microphone stands, an amp on the floor, and an upright piano. A.J. got a beer from the bar (Rolling Rock was the only choice) and sat at a table.

The man stepped to the microphone and said, "Hello, I'm Eric Wood." He began to play. The music was jazzy, blue, mysterious, sung in a smoky tenor that slid through scales like a sax. "Into this heart of mine...came such a voodoo wind...I dared to cross a line...I can't cross back again."

After two beers A.J. decided it was time to leave, but first he had to pee. When he came out of the bathroom, the song Wood was playing caught his interest and he decided to stay longer and listen. He got another beer, but now the tables were all occupied. He saw an empty chair at a table where two women sat. It was out of character, but on an impulse he leaned down close between them so he didn't have to shout, and asked if he could share their table.

He was momentarily intoxicated by musky perfume. They both smiled and nodded, and he took the empty chair. At last, he was beginning to feel better—much better than he had felt all day. As long as he didn't remember who he was, everything was fine.

The man at the microphone plucked his strings in a laid-back syncopation and crooned in a way that had the odd effect of pulling A.J. in, as if floating ever closer, without moving. "I won't try to entice or intrigue you with my darker side...I don't need no seductive confessions, just some honest lies...Soak our souls in our sweat and our sweetness and we won't think twice...Let's pretend that our virtue is weakness and our strength is vice...."

Between songs, A.J. came out of his hypnosis, almost. He chatted with Tia and Sandy, bought beers for the table. Tia was paying him close attention. Her dark hair would often fall in front of her face and he would see her large exotic eyes looking through it at him. When the set was over, Sandy whispered in her friend's ear and got up. She made her way to the bar and shouldered up against Wood with flirty familiarity. Tia said to A.J., "Would you like to get out of here?"

Out on the street in the warm night, they headed east toward Tompkins Square Park, walking so close no light came between them, laughing like old pals. His legs felt liquid, but he didn't say so. They dodged a pair of mohawked punks and entered the park. No trace was left of the homeless camps and anti-gentrification riots of a few years ago, but he felt their ghosts. She took his elbow and pulled him into a shadowy spot under a tree. "I have something for us," she said.

She pulled a pinky-sized vial from her tiny sequined shoulder bag, tapped a bit of white powder onto the back of her hand, and sniffed it up. She offered the vial to A.J.

"Be gentle with me, I'm a cocaine virgin," he said.

She snickered, "Yeah, right." He copied her motions, sniffed it up. She did it again, the other nostril. He followed.

He hadn't known what to expect but soon discovered a monumental rosy pleasure rising, with an undercurrent of urgency that pushed it toward...toward something, he didn't know what. He had to find it, whatever it was. She grabbed his elbow again, took him to the street, they walked and laughed. She kept her hands on his arm, walked close. He let himself be led, steered, like a child.

It seemed he couldn't get the smile off his face, the rictus grin. Now they were sitting at an ill-lit bar, someplace he'd never been. A whiskey ginger tastes damn good, have another. Walking again. Constant conversation had never been so easy. Keep talking, don't stop, can't stop.

Now they were on a subway. Chasing something, but what, who cares, forget it. They heartily disagreed about everything—movies, books, politics—and found their disagreement silly, preposterous. Hilarious! Now they were walking on streets he'd never seen before, 187th, Cabrini. Now they were in a white apartment.

Occasionally a phantom from his day, previous day, previous weeks, a faceless homunculus with malign intent, would rise up like a toothy rodent from a burrow. It was a game of Whack-a-Mole. Ha! Quick! Wield your mallet, knock it back down!

As the night went on it was happening more and more frequently—*knock it down!*—even as he kissed her, even as they scrambled to take each other's clothes from their bodies—*knock it down! knock it down!*—even as they tangled their limbs and pressed their flesh together, even as they each found their own oblivion.

Mercifully, he slept, they slept. Perhaps for mere minutes, certainly not hours, then A.J. found himself rising out of a murky depth with her mouth on his and her hands on his body. She brought out the cocaine again and they each took another snort. *Knock it down, kill it!* Bodies mingled. He saw the wrinkles around her mouth, the crow's feet at her eyes. He knew she saw his mask.

Again they slept, they slept far into the morning. Waking this time was even worse than yesterday. He was clawing his way from a grave, only to find his body still dead. Every movement a wave of pain, like lifting cement blocks with broken bones in every limb. He managed to stand.

Tia sprawled naked on top of the covers, her mouth hanging open and a drool stain on the pillow. Was she dead? She couldn't be dead. She let out a faint snore.

This was when, with no warning, he faced a moment of reckoning. He stood there without mind, naked and nameless, with flaccid penis and softening belly and pale hairy legs, smelly, stupid, blinking. He stared at this sleeping woman he did not know, and at the rumpled bed where he had just lain. And from nowhere there arose a vast swell of rage, a moving mountain of hate. Now. This was it. The final act that everything seemed to point toward. What was mere thought before, could now be made real. This was his chance to get it all over and done with.

On a windowsill near the bed was a stone statuette, a dancing Tara. It was heavy, with sharp edges. The image was vivid in his mind. He would pick the thing up, flexing powerful muscles, raising it high with both hands, smashing it down, down on Tia's head again and again, the crunch of bone, blood spurting across white sheets, again and again and again in wild release until all his fury was spent. Finally, he would be free.

Was this truly who he was? How could that be?

He stood at the foot of the bed and watched her sleep, while at the same time he watched himself confront the monster inside him. On a bright morning in a tastefully furnished room, he wrestled with the darkest horror he had ever known. His hands wanted that stone club. His mind didn't. He trembled. Sweat sprang to his armpits. He struggled to breathe. But he didn't move, minute after minute.

She snored softly again and stirred, the curve of her breast catching light. Then he made his decision, and he acted.

It hurt to move, but he stepped forward, sat on the bed near her, and gently stroked her arm. "Would you like coffee?" he asked.

She shifted again, coughed, and her eyes opened. After a moment, they focused on him, and she groaned. "Please leave," she said.

OUTSIDE IN THE SUNSHINE, A.J. walked in the direction he felt to be south, through streets he'd never seen before. Aching head, sluggish muscles, an alarming twitch in one eyelid. Shoulders hunched and eyes down, he hoped he was invisible. Nobody should see this ugly creature who had such monstrous impulses. To stop replaying the abhorrent moment in his mind, he switched his thoughts to Tia. *I'm sorry*, his inaudible voice said to her intangible presence. *It was not personal.*

Who is she? As he left her apartment, he had seen on the desk by the door a framed snapshot of a man and a laughing girl, a much younger Tia. Next to it was a *New York Times* page with a photo of the same man, older, distinguished, gray at the temples, above the headline, "Iranian Expat Professor Farhad Amouzgar Dies in Hit-and-Run." On the mailboxes in the lobby, under 2B was her name: Tiamat Amouzgar. He brooded as he walked, remembering college mythology lessons: Tiamat...the primordial chaos, the ocean, the mother of unruly gods. Embodied as a fierce dragon, Leviathan. Killed by the noble Marduk (her grandson!), who brought order to the cosmos and created the human race.

None of that gave any clarity to his questions: *What next? Will I see her again?* Nor to the responses: *Are you crazy? After you almost...—! Just chalk it up to experience, you idiot!* Nor to that other voice: *She's probably not interested anyway.*

Enough. He ducked into a bodega to ask where the nearest subway was.

E.3 Even Worse Wednesday

As A.J. ENTERED HIS apartment, his attention was immediately caught by the blinking red light on his answering machine. Five messages! That was unusual for a Wednesday morning. Or rather, afternoon. Then like a wave of something rising in him like vomit, a physical sensation that forced him to sit down, the memory came back: he was supposed to work for I.I.I. today. Call time was seven this morning. He had entirely missed an important gig for his key client.

Dreading what he would hear, he played the messages. They started with Diana's voice, going from gentle inquiry, to concern for his safety, to annoyance. Then it was Hugh's voice, a growl of rage. The last one was like cold steel: "You need to come to the office today at 4pm. Be there."

When he called back, there was no answer. They must still be in production, but would wrap soon. He sat on his bed with his head in his hands for a long time, numb. Then he downed a sandwich and coffee, showered and shaved, mentally rehearsing apologies all the way through.

At four o'clock he entered the I.I.I. offices. The place was empty and dark except for the glow of the three monitors at the editing desk. Hugh sat in profile at the keyboard, shuttling footage. A high-pitched babble at low volume came from the speakers. Hugh spoke without turning. "Give me your key."

A.J. was stunned. He didn't expect that. "Hugh, I'm really sorry. I don't have an excuse, I'm not gonna lie. I fucked up. It won't happen again."

"You're right, it won't." Hugh stopped his tape search, and the room went silent. The two top monitors showed the same man's face from different angles, two views of the same instant, both cameras' tapes locked together by time code. Hugh turned and fixed A.J. with an icy stare. "Diana and I made a policy when we started this business. No show, no call...no mercy."

"But—"

"I don't wanna hear it, A.J." His volume went up a notch. "We've been generous with you, but there are plenty of cameramen in this city. You cost me a lot of stress, money, and good client relations today." He stood and advanced toward A.J. His football past was clear in not only his height and shoulders but the scowl on his face. His hand was out. "Gimme the key."

In a daze, A.J. dug in his pocket, pulled out his keychain, slid the key off, and put it in Hugh's hand. He stood in silence as Hugh sat back down and turned toward the monitors. He rotated the tape shuttle knob a quarter turn, the speakers squawked, and the doctor on the two screens moved his head like a robot an inch to the right, in visual stereo—one in close-up from the front, the other in medium shot from a three-quarters angle. A.J. had the odd sensation of having been behind the camera shooting this footage, behind both cameras in fact, but of course that was impossible; he had been behind neither. Not this time—despite how much it was like so many other times. Something like vertigo threw the room into a sudden tilt, all relationships meaningless, all juxtapositions nonsensical, unrelated heads and faces and furniture and hardware and body parts, a disintegrating Cubist painting, a surreal joke.

"Have a good life." Hugh's flat statement sounded more like "Fuck off." A.J. gathered enough of his wits to turn and leave the room.

Now, for the second time that day, he was walking south with a hunch and frown, eyes inward, paying no attention to the people streaming past. His muddled thoughts fled into abstraction. Two objects are seen, one on each screen. Not faces, just forms. The images are not identical. They have no apparent connection. One moves, the other moves. Simultaneously. Then again. And again. It can't be coincidence. How are they communicating with each other? Does one control the other? How are they entangled?

No, stupid—look below the surface! They are not two things "entangled." They are only one thing! The primordial chaos, the boiling quantum ocean, is the source of all order! See through this phony reality screen like a two-way mirror! Wake up!

There was a liquor store on 6th Avenue near his apartment. He bought a fifth of Bushmills Original, a squeezer of lime juice, and a liter of ginger ale. Maybe he could learn to be a bartender.

THE DAY WAS NOT over yet.

He gathered the mail from his slot in the entryway and tossed it on his kitchen table while he made himself a lukewarm whiskey ginger. On the top envelope he recognized his mother's handwriting. It was thick, likely containing the Mormon propaganda she liked to send him despite his request to cease and desist. *Please, not now*, he thought, and put it aside.

He opened the next envelope. It was a letter from Louise, the acquaintance who held the lease on his apartment. Her upstate situation had fallen apart: a divorce, a move to a different house that turned out to be infested with mold. Now she was couch-surfing with friends. She had no choice: she had to take her apartment back. Soon. She could give him two weeks to vacate.

Two weeks until he'd be homeless.

A.J. emptied the cocktail in one long gulp, then made another and guzzled it as well. *This day needs to be drowned.* He made a third, but without the ginger ale, then punched Play on his stereo and slumped in a chair in his darkening living room. As Chet Baker's "Moon and Sand" from the *Let's Get Lost* soundtrack submerged him in its dark syrupy groove, he sat dead-eyed. The requisite actions could not be taken. The essential muscle was nowhere to be found. To sink was the only motion possible. "Imagination" and "You're My Thrill" floated him on their hypnotic currents. When he stood with empty glass in hand to go to the kitchen for another, his body was liquid, ungovernable. He sat again. *This won't do.* Images began to fill his mind: himself, bearded and dirty, sleeping on cardboard on a subway grate, clutching an empty bottle. Himself, emaciated, shivering behind a dumpster in an alley, fumbling with a syringe and a spoon. Every possible variety of his degraded self swam into view and out again. *This is not me!* But it was.

Somewhere in the middle of the album, he stopped the music. In the silence, he knew what he had to do. He had to get some fucking help. He set his jaw and lurched out the door and down the stairs, setting with determination one foot in front of the other. His destination was several zig-zag blocks to the west: St. Luke's Church on Hudson Street. He had walked past there a few times and seen a sign about AA meetings, with people entering or exiting a side door, down a walkway through a lovely little garden. That was what he needed.

The shadows were long but the city no less busy and loud as he crossed Hudson at Grove Street, dodged a pedestrian, and strode without hesitation through the open gate in the tall wrought-iron fence. He headed down the narrow walk lined with flowers, into the church's side yard, past two guys smoking and a couple chatting on a bench, his blunt, drunken focus only on the cream-colored door where the meetings must be held. Surely there would be one in progress right now.

But then, without his conscious command, his feet stopped. What was he doing? He had no idea. For a moment he stood slack-jawed, eyes on the ground. He did an abrupt about-face.

That's when he saw Ashton Gill. Turning from the sidewalk into the churchyard gate was the man who had appeared in the nighttime photo A.J. had given to Felicity, the same man he'd encountered long ago in a Jersey City diner. In a sudden flood of knowledge, A.J. understood: the guy was following him. This was the creep! The author! This was the monster who'd been stalking him, invading his mind, writing those stories, stealing his life!

A.J.'s mindless body was already in motion, lunging forward, fist clenched, arm cocked, a strangled roar in his throat. He swung at the man's startled face, missed, stumbled, turned and charged again, both fists wild. He connected with a parrying arm but felt an explosion of pain in his side. He swiveled, lunged again, flailing in blind rage, and a second blast of pain seared his gut just before a sledgehammer slammed between his eyes and the world went black.

E.4 Does It Hurt?

RISING WITH A TRAILING wake of dread, up from a dark murky soup of half-formed images and scrambled words, up into cold light and the odor of antiseptic, A.J. was startled to see before anything else the face of the man who had knocked him unconscious. He jerked back against the half-upright bed, felt a spear of pain pierce his ribs, then watched with surprise as the man leaned forward and looked with apparent concern into his eyes.

"Don't worry, everything is okay," the man said. He was exactly as A.J. remembered Ashton Gill—same tanned features with a day's growth of stubble, same shoulder-length brown hair, same jeans and white shirt—but he spoke with a thick accent.

"I will not hurt you," he said. The accent was...maybe Spanish. "I was only defending myself. The witnesses agreed, and the police did not arrest me. So, I came here to see how you are doing."

A.J.'s vision was blurry at the edges. His head hurt. He had dim, distorted flashes of memory: an ambulance ride, an X-ray machine, a young doctor with glasses. Pain.

The man continued: "You have a broken rib and a broken nose. Not serious. But I am very sorry to hurt you. You surprised me, and I reacted as I am trained."

"Who are you?" A.J. didn't recognize his own voice: a nasal croak.

"I am Gilberto Cineza. I am from Spain, but I have lived in New York for almost ten years." His smile was kind as he said, "I make my living as a Mixed Martial Arts master, so you see, you did not have a chance to hurt me."

A.J. groaned. "Just my luck." He gently touched his face. Now he understood that the fuzzy whiteness between his eyes was a bandage covering a splint on his nose. His nostrils were plugged; he had to keep his mouth open to breathe. But he couldn't breathe deeply or his torso would feel like it was splitting.

Ceniza leaned back in his bedside chair. "Why did you attack me?"

"I must have gone crazy. I thought you were someone else." A.J. still felt dimwitted, as if his skull was stuffed with cotton. But he knew he didn't want to explain; he still didn't entirely trust what he was hearing. This guy's physical resemblance to Ashton Gill was just too perfect. They were doppelgangers. Identical twins.

A nurse swept in carrying a plastic tub. "Ah, very good, you're awake. I'm going to ice that rib again. And we've decided to keep you here until morning, let that booze wear off." She looked at him over her glasses as she smoothly untied his gown at the back of his neck. She slipped it down over his left arm and revealed an ugly bruise across his midsection. When she placed a towel and an ice pack on it, A.J. flinched. "Ouch!"

"This will help, and tomorrow we'll send you home with some pain meds. But no drinking." She put his arm back in the gown sleeve.

Ceniza stood up. "I am going to leave now, Angus. Or is it James?"

"A.J."

"Okay, A.J., I must go home now. It is very late. I would like to visit you tomorrow afternoon to see how you are doing."

"That's not necessary." A.J. hated the thought of being home alone in this condition, but he wouldn't let that show.

"But I would like to."

"I'll be back in a few minutes," the nurse said. "Just relax." She bustled out.

Ceniza pulled a miniature notebook and a pen from his back pocket. "*Por favor*, here, write your address and phone."

A.J. complied. He seemed to have very little will of his own. But more than that, he was ravenous with curiosity.

ALTHOUGH HE LOVED TO walk the Village, A.J. was happy the next morning to take a cab the few blocks from St. Vincent's Hospital to his apartment. The stairs were a challenge, met with resolute focus. He spent the next hours ruminating with despair on the new burden of hospital bills on top of his new immobility, his new joblessness, his imminent homelessness. Beneath the despair glowed the familiar ember of repressed fury, threatening to burst into flame. He swallowed ibuprofen with lots of water and resisted the urge for alcohol. He napped.

It was midafternoon when he was surprised by the buzzer that signaled that rare event: a guest at the street door, requesting access. To get out of the chair, he needed to use his arms and legs, with no help from his stomach muscles. Not easy.

When Cineza entered, he was holding the hand of a small boy who looked much like him. "This is my son, Arturo. I just picked him up from school," he said. Arturo appeared to be about the same age as Max. He gazed at A.J. with his father's observant, thoughtful stare, then stepped forward with his hand out. "Hello, sir."

"Hello, Arturo, pleased to meet you." A.J. was suddenly filled with emotion as, in one instant, he recognized the damage that had been done to his own children by their warring parents. He blinked back tears, shook Arturo's hand, offered them seats.

"We cannot stay, A.J." Cineza said. "Just wanted to see how you are doing. Do you need anything?"

"Ha. Do I." A.J. attempted a grin, but he knew it was more of a grimace. "Well, there's a long list, but no. I appreciate your offer."

"Okay. Well, here is what we are going to do," Cineza said with firmness. *Odd that he looks like Harrison Ford but sounds like Antonio Banderas*, A.J. thought. "I will come by tomorrow morning at eight o'clock and take you to breakfast. You will need to walk with me, which I know is good for your injuries. So sleep well tonight." He turned to go.

Arturo did not follow his father. He gestured toward A.J.'s face, the black eyes, the splint and bandage. "Does it hurt, sir?"

"Thank you for asking, Arturo. Yes, sometimes it does. But soon it will heal."

"Yes, sir. I know it will. And your other hurts will heal too." The boy's open gaze held A.J.'s own, kind and steady.

This time, A.J. could not hold back. His eyes brimmed with tears. He could not speak, could only nod and attempt a smile, and nod again as the man and boy turned and went out the door.

Later, as he heated up a can of soup for dinner, the dull ache in his midsection seemed to be speaking to him—something about the tragedy of families, all families. They never turn out like one's hopes and dreams. People change. He remembered how his mother in old photos looked as beautiful as a movie star, and how her laugh rang out as free and high as a child's when they played board games all together. She had been his friend, his confidant, his only support when he faced the terrors of elementary school. So many times she had told him, "I'm proud of you."

He decided it was time to open the letter she'd sent. The envelope was thick because, in addition to two folded sheets of paper, it contained a cassette tape. The tape was not in a case and looked as if it had been run over by a truck: the plastic shell was cracked into several pieces. The cassette was completely unplayable. On the label, in his mother's elegant hand, were the words, "Elder Packer's speech on fatherhood." A.J.'s immediate reaction was relief that he would not need to listen to the tape nor to lie about it. He could just tell her it was destroyed in the mail.

As he ate his soup, he read her letter. She addressed him not by his name but with the phrase, "My dearest son." *You mean your only son*, he thought. As usual, she shared "news"—this time about his young cousin who had won a local bowling championship—shared because, she said, "I know you always liked bowling." *On the contrary, I have never bowled in my entire life*, he silently retorted. He had lied to her a couple of times in high school, claiming he was bowling with a church youth group when, in truth, he'd been out on a hillside with hoodlum friends, getting drunk on Bacardi and Coke. *You don't know me at all. You only know your fantasy of me—the perfect Mormon boy.*

Her letter closed with "Please listen to the tape. Remember, you'll always be my precious firstborn. I pray for Heavenly Father to watch over you. Love, Mom."

Fuck off!

A.J. stared into his empty soup bowl. He hated the voice he was hearing in his own head. It was a petulant child, a rebellious teenager, an ungrateful asshole. It was time to kick this person out, to dig up this thorny, poisonous weed by the roots.

How do I get to the roots? I don't know.

The half-full bottle of Bushmills sat on the counter, calling him. In one motion, he stood, grabbed the bottle, and poured the brown liquid down the sink drain. He dropped the empty bottle into the trash, pulled the liter of ginger ale from the fridge, and poured it down the drain as well. *So be it.*

For a while he stared at his battered face in the bathroom mirror, a stranger, a masked alien, barely familiar. He took acetaminophen, alternating as instructed. He noticed that he had no more interest in the stories in the stack of literary journals, nor about their author. He lay in darkness, listening to jazz, refusing to let his mind follow the channels of worry eroded into his neurons. Sometime in the middle of the night, he awoke from a troubling dream and fumbled his way to a pen and an empty journal page.

E.5 "The Creature," from A.J.'s Dream Log

I HAVE BEEN FIRED from an important corporate job at a newspaper or magazine. Apparently, I have done something deeply, morally wrong, or perhaps I am of generally low character. No details are available; I am humiliated. This news organization is focused on getting at the seed of darkness that ails society; it seems to be common knowledge that such a thing exists, and we can find it. Stories circulate about a wild man-like creature—part hairy ape, part scaly fish—lurking at the edge of town, destroying fences, stealing chickens, scaring children.

This beast must be to blame for everything. The name of the creature seems to be something like "Eager," but the letters are oddly jumbled. I think I know where to look for him, so I get my "weapon"—a complicated contraption that looks a little like a large pistol but also like a camera, and it hangs at my side like a sword—and head out into the wilderness, which means I walk out the back door of my childhood home, into the empty fields beyond, toward the hills in the distance. Soon I find it: a hidden cove in the sandstone cliffs where a narrow waterfall tumbles thirty feet into a deep pool. I recognize this as Lower Calf Creek Falls, a place I visited many times in my youth, but in the dream, it feels like a secret place. I build a campfire on the little sandy beach by the water. It seems that I sit there for many days and nights, burning sticks and watching the pool, my weapon ready. But the little pool is now a big deep lake. Nothing happens, but I am sure that what I am looking for is under the water.

Maybe the creature does not like my weapon, so I disassemble it into many small pieces. The pieces look exactly like the little plastic soldiers and war props that I played with as a child, and I scatter them across the ground. Nothing happens.

It occurs to me that I should disguise myself. I take ashes from the campfire and smear them all over my face and hands, so I no longer look human. I lie on the ground, just a pile of ash. I can get no more invisible than this. Still nothing happens.

It appears my project is a failure. I wade into the water to wash off the ashes, and soon I find myself underwater, naked, walking on the bottom of the lake. I wonder how I can breathe and discover that the sides of my neck are covered in delicate, feathery structures that I realize are gills. I have webs between my fingers.

This seems like a good place to hide. There are many shadowy places, caves and grottoes, reeds and ferns. I'll stay here, and I'll keep looking. I'll keep looking for the mysterious, dangerous man-beast who ruins everything.

E.6 Friday Morning at the Diner

THE NEXT MORNING WAS clear and cool. The day was Friday, the Friday of the worst week A.J. had ever experienced. He walked with careful steps at the side of this stranger, Gilberto Cineza, from his apartment on Jones Street up to West 4th, then across to the

Washington Square Diner on the far side of Sixth Avenue. His silly-looking nose gear felt like a Halloween mask.

They walked and talked.

He learned that Gilberto grew up in the ancient city of Granada, Spain, in the southern region—Andalusia.

"Ah...of which I know nothing except *Un Chein Andalou*, Buñuel and Dali," A.J. said.

"The old Spanish saying is 'When the Andalusian dog howls, someone has died.'" Gilberto said with a chuckle. "Of course, it is the perfect title because it has nothing to do with the movie."

Gilberto had moved to New York to pursue work in the film industry as a martial arts coach. He had not been interested in Los Angeles, feeling that New York would offer much more cultural richness. When he said "New York is the center of the world," it echoed in A.J.'s memory. Hadn't Ashton said the same thing?

Gilberto had married a young woman from Ireland who did props and wardrobe for the theater. He supplemented his occasional movie and TV jobs by teaching Mixed Martial Arts classes, one of the first teachers of that fighting style. His background was in karate first, but he had deeply explored kung fu, taekwondo, aikido, even capoeira.

At the diner, they sat in a booth next to a window looking out at sunlight filtering through a tiny grove of trees. *A much better view than the bleak midnight parking lot of the Tunnel Diner*, A.J. thought. He couldn't help comparing this diner visit to the one when he met Ashton Gill five years ago, as if these impossible twins were indeed the same person. That thought arose repeatedly, although it was absurd. After all, Gilberto had his hair pulled back into a ponytail today, and his ears looked entirely normal.

A waitress appeared; they ordered breakfast and continued their conversation.

"I'm curious," A.J. said. "There's a desert plant called Purple Sage or Texas Silverleaf, but it's also called Cineza—your name. Why is that?"

"Yes, I know about it. Probably because of the color of the leaves. My name means 'ash' or 'cinders.'"

"Ash."

"Yes."

The twinning just wouldn't stop. A.J. kept a poker face. "Okay. What does 'Gilberto' mean?"

Gilberto laughed. "Bright lad."

"But it has the syllable 'gil' in it."

"Yes."

"Gill. Ash. Evocative words."

Gilberto smiled. "What do the words 'Angus James Campbell' mean?"

"I can tell you more about *your* name. I remember reading Norse mythology—the very first man was Askr, which means 'ash.' And a giant ash tree is the *axis mundi*, the stem that goes from the underworld to the heavens, around which the entire cosmos revolves."

"Good to know."

"But about *my* name, I have no idea."

"You are a mystery to yourself, *mi amigo*. This calls for a journey within."

"Hmm, maybe you can help. Let me tell you a dream I had."

Their breakfast arrived as A.J. was finishing his tale of the man-beast dream. They began to eat without speaking. Gilberto nodded and chewed as he pondered what he had heard. Minutes passed with nothing but the clink of silverware. Then he said,

"Well, *mi sentido*, my sense, is that you already know the meaning of this dream. The journey toward manhood includes being brought down from a high place to a low place—this is what ashes represent: sacrifice, penitence, grief. The burning down of your dreams, but also the chance that a phoenix might arise. Possibly also, from a Jungian point of view, ashes relate to the Shadow archetype—the things you hate most about yourself."

A.J. stared into his coffee cup as he listened. Gilberto kept speaking, his voice smooth and musical.

"And you probably already know that large bodies of water represent the subconscious mind. Gills are like scuba gear—the tools you need to stay alive underwater. So they allow you to explore your subconscious *extensamente*, at length, to become self-aware—a very important step if you want to be a man, not a boy.

"The weapon—the camera-gun that is also the child's toy, a toy that is uniquely masculine in our warlike culture—these are just signature props, as are the locations from your childhood. They say: this is A.J.'s dream, nobody else's."

Without looking up, A.J. asked: "What about the beast?" Or maybe he only thought it. He wasn't sure his mouth had moved. Gilberto kept talking.

"The creature is *la materia*, or you might say, the stuff, of many classic folktales. The Wild Man of the Forest: dangerous, but a teacher. The rugged, untamed part of us that has grown beyond our mother's control. A man's strength, his earth wisdom, his warrior nature—but also perhaps his darkness, his downfall. *Debes llevarlos a los dos*...you must carry them both.

"But remember, all this is just my *interpretación*—and is, you know, generic. This dream was your personal message. What the creature represents for you—that is for you to figure out on your own."

As Gilberto spoke, A.J. felt himself retreat into a solitary chamber where nothing seemed to exist except Gilberto's hypnotic voice. The circle that was his empty coffee cup filled his vision. His thoughts had begun to reel out in sync with Gilberto's words, and soon, A.J. was only hearing his own self.

Do I know what the beast is? Of course I know. I told myself I didn't know how to dig out the spiteful, ugly voice by its roots like a weed. But I lied. I do know. Of course I know.

The voice had begun to make itself clear after the death of his father. He was not yet twelve then; his world was demolished. How could life go on without his father? The absence was unfathomable. But his mother just said things like: "Heavenly Father has taken him home." "He's in a better place now." "He's with Jesus; at last he'll be happy."

And she said things like: "Jimmy, you're our big strong man now." "Jimmy, you're so good, what a wonderful priesthood leader you will be." "Jimmy, you're my gift from God."

He hated everything she said. It was all lies.

And then, within a year, she was married again. The man she married was the opposite of his father: corpulent, verbose. He was a widower from their congregation, a man who made a show of his dedication to the doctrines, his righteous labor in church callings, his vast spiritual wisdom. He would affect a theatrically deep tone and slow delivery whenever he spoke (frequently) on religious topics.

Twelve-year-old A.J. boiled inside.

That is the root of my rage. That's when it began.

But no...it was just the angry voice that began then, the boy's silent voice spewing hateful words at his mother. The inarticulate rage itself—that was even deeper and older. Something pre-verbal, infantile, flailing limbs, bellowing lungs, the battle against helplessness, against giants, against all restraint. The life-or-death struggle for autonomy, to own one's own body. To make one's own way. To write one's own story.

I was fucking furious on the day I was born. It's my steady-state reality, the background of everything.

In the diner, all this happened in a waking dream, no time reckoned, swirling in an empty cup in front of A.J.'s staring eyes.

I am fucking furious. See it. Nothing needs to be done. Don't act. Just know.

"Would you like a refill?" It was a young woman's voice.

A.J. looked across the table. There was no trace of Gilberto. He looked up at the waitress. She was not the same woman who had served them before.

"Did my friend leave?" he asked.

"I don't know, sir, I just started my shift. I didn't see anyone, but your check has been paid." Her name tag said *Alegria*. She lifted the coffee pot.

"No, thanks—I'll be leaving now."

She walked away and A.J. stood up slowly, moving with care to avoid pain. Just before he pushed open the door to the outside, he turned back and made his way to where Alegria was pouring coffee for a couple in a booth.

"May I ask what your name means?" he said.

She smiled shyly. "It's Spanish for happiness."

"Ah, of course it is. Thank you."

As A.J. shuffled toward home, the morning sunshine couldn't pierce his reverie about the inexplicable echoes between the two versions of one man, the two visits to diners, the explications of meaning in his life, all separated in time by five-plus years. Could his memory be trusted? Could his sanity be trusted?

He pondered the insight he'd found. Could he simply gaze at his anger, acknowledge its existence—*oh, there you are again*—but not act on it? Could he be a conscious man?

The reverie only lasted a few minutes, and then his dire life circumstances loomed up again. He began to visualize his near future: circling newspaper ads for an affordable apartment (needle/haystack), calling potential clients and industry contacts, hoping his reputation wasn't ruined...and then, if his two weeks ran out with no luck, making all his outgoing calls from phone booths, hiring an answering service, letting his contacts know the change, getting a storage facility or maybe keeping some of his stuff at Felicity's place, sleeping in his car until he could get something better, eating on the cheap, counting every penny. All the while, trying not to let his kids, or his ex, know the depths to which he'd fallen.

He will see them on Sunday, the day after tomorrow. "There was an accident at work," he'll say. Stick to the story, no detail. Hope they'll be kind.

He considered returning the literary journals to Molly. How could he care any longer about the unsolvable mystery of the invisible author? Chasing a phantom is a luxury. Real life takes one's full attention.

It was a beautiful morning. All this torture would pass. Or would it?

E.7 "Another War," a Short Story by Robbie Brand

WHEN THE BOMBING STARTED, J.T. Carter was deep in the bowels of a bank in Baltimore with a video camera on his shoulder, capturing, *cinema verité*, the mundane fate of everyone's rent check.

Machine-clatter filling his ears, he stared through the lens at a shuffling deck of personal checks, a non-stop riffling flow like the first flourish of a magician's card trick, but without end and performed by fingerless giants built of plastic and steel. Across the room, the girl running the Damaged Item Sorter removed her radio earphones and announced over the rushing roar of a river of money, "Bush done it. He's whuppin' 'em."

J.T. never took his eye from the viewfinder, just zoomed in a little tighter on the beautiful leafy flutter of paper in the grip of the rattling machine.

Later, at dinner with the video crew at a Hungarian restaurant, J.T. observed as if from outside his body as Gloria, the brunette actress who played the bank's spokeswoman, flirted overtly with him. It was more than just the joking camaraderie that had grown between them during the day. At dessert, she stood behind him and rubbed his shoulders and neck. He stared at the tablecloth, enjoying her touch, but embarrassed. Meanwhile, the waiter, a lugubrious but talkative Eastern European, told in his thick accent, wide-eyed with fear, about his younger brother who was in the U.S. Army somewhere near Kuwait. The crew sat silent or fidgeting.

J.T. hadn't had sex in nearly two years. This was January; his divorce had been final last June, after a year of bruising court battles and depressed waiting. For months before that there had been nothing between him and his wife, no kissing, no touching, almost no speaking.

Now he was bitterly lonely. In many ways, his life was great; he enjoyed his work as never before, after making a career change a year previous. He had left a corporate accounting job to tackle the world of freelance photography, both still and video. He had even revised his identity; he was no longer Jeff (short for Jefferson) T. (for Thaddeus) Carter, named for stern ancestors in sepia photos. "J.T." looked so much better on his new business cards, and he liked how it sounded in the mouths of art directors and communications managers, his clients. After six months of struggle, the new venture had finally begun to pay his bills, as long as he lived modestly. He felt he had found a sort of balance. But he still lived alone in a tiny drab apartment and had no social life except with his kids (daughter six, son four; fun but not exactly socially fulfilling). He was desperate to be caressed.

Also, there was a truth that J.T. was embarrassed about: he had never had sex with anyone but his ex-wife. Back home in rural Utah, in a family of faithful Mormons, that's what was expected: marry young, as virgins, then be monogamous forever. For all of eternity. Even after he'd left that religion behind, come to live in the capital of worldliness, New York City, and wound up single, still his experience with any other woman's body was limited to the occasional magazine and masturbatory fantasy.

He wanted that situation to change. A few weeks earlier, on a shoot in Fort Lauderdale, he'd gone alone to a strip club and dropped a hundred bucks on sodas for a blonde with a Dutch accent and muscular thighs, watching her dance naked on his table. Later she'd met him at a coffee shop, told him all about her life, then walked away, leaving him with nothing to do but watch the sun rise on the beach until time for his flight back to New York.

So, after dinner, when Gloria whispered in his ear, "Come to my room," he knew he would go. She was no more than a new acquaintance, with whom he had little in common, but he knew he would go.

Two hours later he hung in a tilting limbo, at once both pleasured and split. They had turned on the hotel TV; war news on all channels. They had chatted, kissed, were suddenly naked on the bed, his fingertips on her skin like latte silk, exquisite, smelling fresh from a shower. Her nipples were large and dark, and he thought of gulping rich, sweet coffee, nothing like his ex-wife's, those sips of pale rose tea. And on TV, Desert Storm was in full swing! Who inhabited his body, doing this? Not himself, not himself. How could such opposites co-exist? Fresh-faced news anchors praising with pride the capabilities of America's "smart" Patriot missiles—intelligent target-seeking! pinpoint accuracy!—and gravely condescending to those pathetic Iraqi "Scuds," and the screen showing explosions in cheery green with a video-camera frame like a cross between home movies and Nintendo, and casualties counting up on candy-colored bar-charts like votes, and the sound of war as entertainment blaring on and on and on. And yet, and yet, here was a man—surely just a generic man, nameless, without history, a silly man—making urgent, fumbling love to a stranger in a hotel room in Baltimore. How could anything be real?

They didn't speak. Her eyes stayed closed.

Afterward, they shut the TV off and in the blessed silence remembered the fun they'd had working together. He was glad they could return to that and shut everything else out. She clowned, miming the producer's imaginary shocked reaction to this illicit employee rendezvous. They laughed a lot, then it was a quick kiss and an exaggerated play of stealth as he snuck out of her room to go back to his own and sleep.

The next morning, J.T. said goodbye to Gloria and the rest of the video crew as they left for New York. He felt raw, as if his skin had been scraped, and he didn't know how to speak to anyone, especially her. What did it mean? A new relationship? Another tour of duty in the battle zone of love? No? Then why not?

He feared he'd been a disappointment the night before, yet she seemed to like him a lot, and there was no doubt he'd enjoyed her body. She was pretty and fun; he liked her. But she hadn't spoken her feelings. What do New Yorkers do? He wasn't one yet, not really. He was a Utah boy, and back in that world, there is no such thing as casual sex. Sex is a sacred manifestation of eternal love. Or, if not that, at least genuine relationship. Was he ready for that? Again? Or was this all just too dangerous?

He covered his turmoil with smiles and a stolen twinkle of eye contact with her, and the crew drove away. In that tiny glance was an agreement: yes, he'd be seeing her again, and his heart did a little happy dance. Even so, now he was relieved to be alone, alone to follow his plan: drive an hour to Washington DC, see the Paul Strand photography exhibit at the National Gallery, submerge himself in images, be simple, learn something real.

STRAND WAS ONE OF the mythic figures, the early giants of photography as a fine art, a pioneer from the days when the world must have been black and white. J.T. wandered as if in a meditation through the hushed, empty gallery rooms, where each warm-toned monochrome print hung in its own spotlight. Some were abstracts of form and line, shadow and light, close-up studies of everyday objects that turned them to classical architecture. Others were street portraits, faces of the rugged, the weathered, the poor, the workers of the world, images driven by the leftist politics that led Strand to become an expatriate at the dawn of the McCarthy era.

J.T. loved the fact that Strand had invented a sideways-shooting camera that could appear to be focused in one direction while shooting another, allowing him to capture his subject unaware, unposed, authentic. And he had pioneered documentary filmmaking as well: a man who crossed genres, linked across time in kinship with J.T., or with J.T.'s dreams of himself.

Hours passed. It felt to J.T. as if he were in a temple, his own private worship space, and he was fully immersed in seeing, thinking, absorbing into his body the perfect stillness and silence, the form, line, tone, and wordless meanings of the images. Eventually he was full and made his way out of the Strand show into the huge, vaulted lobby of the National Gallery and then out through the glass doors into the bright winter sunshine.

He walked from quiet into chaos. It had not occurred to him that the Mall would be crowded, packed from the Washington Monument to the Capitol with demonstrators—a noisy, colorful maelstrom, a circus of political viewpoints, people shouting,

singing, handing out buttons and flyers—the whole gamut of ide-
ologies, from the yellow ribbon crusaders to those who demanded
we assassinate Bush and spare poor Saddam. Vietnam vets, tie-dyed
teenagers, spiky punks, frisbees and dogs and 12-foot puppets on
parade, music everywhere, and under it all a vibration of desperate
anger, violence barely in check, hatred under the sun in a scene like
some upside-down Woodstock.

J.T. stood stunned for a moment as if on the bank of a raging
river, then he gripped the camera dangling from his neck and
plunged in. For a half hour he operated on instinct and adrenaline,
grabbing pictures through his wide-angle as the moments presented themselves, squinting, crouching, this way, that, everything on
the fly, humans of every sort flowing in a loud, spastic current over
him then gone.

But his energy couldn't last. Something bubbled up from his
heart and he suddenly stopped amidst the shouts and songs and
anger, images of his children in his head along with utter bewilderment. How could it be that in twenty years America had come no
further than this? How could we have learned nothing, nothing
at all, from the horror of Vietnam? The whole scene was insane,
impossible, a terrible recurring nightmare from which there was
no escape. He fled.

DRIVING UP 95 TOWARD home, J.T.'s thoughts were a jumble:
still, silvery forms bathed in spectral light; angry faces, wild motion and blaring sound; dreamlike memories of the night before,
Gloria's skin, hair, laughter, the sweetness of touching. Explosions.
Bullet tracers in night-vision green. A blind beggar's face in crisp

sepia. Swirling flags, red-white-blue, peace chants and violent ges-
tures. Deep, long kisses. Something big was happening to him.
What did it all mean? His throat too full, he switched on the radio.
A mistake. Nothing but dull reportage of death and atrocities in
monotone voices, droning on. That was when, glazed eyes on the
road, he slipped into the past.

*I am running, running down a rutted, mountain road, endlessly
running and shouting, "Help! Help! My dad is hurt!"*

*It is summer, 1973, and I am eleven years old, helping my dad
with the sheep up on Boulder Mountain like I do every year. He is
only 42, despite his craggy face like an old photograph and his limp
from a sniper's bullet. We are in the meadow near the camp wagon,
and he has suddenly fallen to the ground, grabbing his left arm,
moaning, eyes rolled up, pupils invisible. He won't talk to me; I can't
pick him up; I don't know what to do, I just run, run and cry and y
ell.*

*My dad is a strong man, a farmer, a veteran of the Korean War,
a survivor of the useless slaughter at Pork Chop Hill. A man with
strong opinions but very few words. After a hard day's work and
a silent dinner, he would sit and watch the 10 O'Clock News, a
scary dark frown on his brow, and mutter "goddamn bastards" over
and over. But I knew he wasn't talking about the Viet Cong. He
was talking about the generals and politicians and corporate bosses
getting rich while young men bled and died in the muddy jungles.
He didn't care much for hippies and their protests, but he cared even
less about military pride. When we pulled out of the war that spring,
he grunted and nodded at the TV, as happy as I'd ever seen him.*

*I stumble and fall, scraping my palms on stones. I get up and run. I
run until I think my heart and lungs will burst out of my chest, then
I walk a little while, then I run again. When I get to the ranger's*

station, it's almost sunset. My breath is hoarse. I can barely walk or talk, but I say what I need to. As we race in his Jeep back up the bumpy road to the sheep camp, I struggle to keep from sobbing. I know we're too late, I knew it all along.

I had heard the terrible groans from deep in my father's chest, and then I had seen his lip quiver and heard him moan like a little child. And I had heard that last thing, a small mournful sigh that said all hope was forever gone, and then the words, "Oh no. Not another war."

J.T. TWITCHED, SWERVED, STOMPED on the brake as a carload of teenagers careened around him, cut him off by inches, loud music thumping, and sped off down an exit ramp. A hand out the window flipped him the finger. They were yelling, laughing, kids having fun. Eyes suddenly blurry, he wrestled his car to a skidding stop on the side of the highway, heart thumping from the nearness of death. Those teens were who he'd been way back when; they were what his children would soon become. How many in that car would die in a foreign desert, for nothing? Were his children facing a future of bleak struggle, of poisoned water, brown air, endless endless war?

He switched off the radio and leaned his head on the steering wheel, trying and trying to stop his thoughts, to think about nothing but the beauty of art and the imminent possibility of new love, until finally his shaking hands grew calm. He wiped the tears from his eyes and looked up. The road ahead was empty. He put his car in gear, checked his mirrors, and stepped on the gas.

F. The Writer

F.1 At Long Last, Your Pitiful Confession

ALL YOUR KIND NEIGHBORS think you're a writer, but you're not. You're a fraud.

Now you sit alone in this steamy, winterless place, feeling tired and used up. Storm clouds are rolling in. It's time to stop the lying.

It began with plagiarism. You were a kid. You found a story and claimed it as your own. It got published, against all odds. Out of nowhere, to you, a befuddled loser, came success.

With a ballpoint pen, you copied those first words—*I can't sleep, although it's dawn*—and the future was made. It's been that way ever since: a story comes to you—from somewhere else, not from your mind—and you write it down and pretend you created it. That first time, it arrived on paper, on a physical medium, but every story after that has come out of the ether—not the internet—arriving through your fingers on the keyboard. The stories seem no different, no more truly your own, than did that first one, scribbled on yellow paper in a stranger's handwriting.

And along with each story comes a disorienting intimacy. Now you *know* them, these people whose private bedrooms you're creeping into, know them almost as well as you know yourself...but they have no idea you're there.

By some blessed quirk of fate, you never met the man whose path, whose story, first crossed yours in such an important way. Important to *you*, that is. To him, too? You don't know. He and his wife were already in the midst of a divorce before you entered the scene.

A family falling apart, the Angus James Campbell family (of course, "all names changed to protect the innocent"—as if anyone innocent exists, ha!). The family you knew more about than you ever should have known. Your "writing career" may have gone no further than the first petty plagiarism if you hadn't felt a compulsion to knock on their door that day in June.

So now you are willing to confess: yes, you slept with another man's wife, the man to whom, perhaps, you owe your identity, your career. Campbell was doubly betrayed, by both you and her.

You faced his wife, but you never had to face A.J. Campbell in person. You slithered away just in time. A few years went by, and then Campbell suddenly started inquiring about "Robbie Brand" through one of your editors. You grew very afraid. Did you not really know him like you thought you did? Was he a violent man? You thought you could throw him off your scent, pull a switcheroo, so one day you anonymously sent to Molly a package full of your publications—a copy of every lit mag where Robbie Brand had published a Campbell story, a half-dozen by that point. Of course, she would think they were written by A.J., and he would assume they were written by her. What kind of fireworks would that set off? Maybe it would be a diversion and you could escape. Did it work? You don't know.

Some of the A.J. stories hold a rosy spot in your memory. There was the one you once felt was your best, if you can take any credit at all. You called it "Another War" and it seemed a heartfelt cry in the night, from a man barely able to ride the wave of changes in his life. And then there was the last story of A.J. that came through to you, before you lost reception from him forever: "The Seed," a concise glimpse into the subtleties of how lives change.

But all that was more than a decade ago, and you never could have imagined all the things that came later. The people whose lives you've exploited for your own gain deserve an apology, but you know you'll never give it to them. You had no choice. The universe offered those people's stories to you free and gratis; you didn't ask. The words and images came streaming into you from somewhere out there, you'll never know where. Who were you to reject such a gift, such a magical endowment?

And how were you to know it was a gift you couldn't handle?

Ah, New York City...the crushing chaos of humanity, the pandemonium of stories—it was just too much. Your sanity grew dangerously thin. You wandered the streets mumbling and twitching.

At the turn of the millennium, before the towers fell, you fled. You landed far away: New Orleans, a foreign land that you gradually grew to love. And you became ever more crafty at covering your tracks.

As the years went by, you wrestled with your cursed gift and the publications rolled in. There were stories, then books, books that actually sold...numerous pseudonyms, various genres...the readings, the occasional teaching gig...they all put a little food on the table and a little salve on the ego. But at what cost?

The bare truth is that you found a story, you stole it, and you became someone new. From that point on, your former self was lost. You became some sort of impossible amalgam of yourself and...the "author," whoever that may be. You became a freak, a two-headed man. Like Borges in "Borges and I," you don't know which of you is writing these words.

It all connects to that thing you learned about back in college physics, a phenomenon physicists have long labored to explain: *quantum entanglement*, in which two subatomic particles are invisibly linked across impossible spaces. They are twins: change one, the other changes too. It made Einstein nervous and he called it "spooky action at a distance." These are the particles of which all of us and everything else are made, and the spooky twinning effect can be scaled up from micro to macro. It applies especially to the *observer* and the *observed*—you and whatever you give your attention to.

So it's clear: you're no writer. You're just easily entangled.

F.2 "The Seed," Flash Fiction by Robbie Brand

THERE ONCE WAS A young man who lied to himself. "I am a corporate accountant" was one of his lies. Another was "I can give up my dreams for the sake of my family."

It is June 1987. Right now, he sits in an airliner far above the American heartland, heading east. He looks at them: pretty young wife in the aisle seat, infant son in her arms, toddler daughter in the seat between. They all sleep peacefully as he watches. "Here is my life," he thinks. Inside his chest is something warm and vast that he identifies as love.

The last two days had been spent with his family of origin: mother, stepfather, two younger sisters, aunts, uncles, cousins. The occasion was his sister's marriage. His stepfather had offered to pay the expenses for him to bring his little tribe "home" to Utah from New Jersey so he could be the wedding photographer. He had tried to politely decline, saying "I'm so out of practice lately." But his sister and mother and stepfather wouldn't listen. As long as he still had that fancy 35mm SLR kit with several lenses and a good flash unit, they were sure he could do it. The whole family knew him as the kid with the camera at every gathering. In high school it was often a Super-8 movie camera.

At their arrival, he was surprised by his own pride and pleasure: the four of them seen through others' eyes. "Oh, what a sweet, beautiful family!" his Aunt Eileen exclaimed, cradling each of their faces in both her palms, one after the other. "Well done," said his Uncle Jack, and slapped him on the back. He shared a secret happy smile with his wife.

But the photography made him nervous. He was genuinely uncertain whether he would screw it all up, and he wouldn't know the results until all the film got processed. He had just been using an Instamatic for snapshots of his kids—that was all the photography he ever did these days. His serious camera gear had been in its bag on the floor of his closet, untouched for years. He had done his best to forget the painful fights during their first year together, when his pregnant teenage wife had demanded his full attention. "The camera or me," she had said. He did what he believed was right, for love.

For the sake of family, the wedding assignment could not be refused. They had flown from Newark to Las Vegas, rented a car, driven north to St. George, Utah, and spent the night in a motel. The next morning, they met the small family group that was attending the official ceremony in the St. George LDS Temple. The young man and his wife had not had this sort of elite Mormon wedding, which takes place in the sacred windowless confines of a temple, off limits to cameras and to people not deemed worthy—they had stopped participating in church activities years earlier, much to the dismay of his mother and stepfather. But his sister and her returned-missionary fiancé were not such apostates.

The photography began outside on the steps of the temple, when everyone who had been inside at the ceremony stood in a group and smiled at the camera in the desert sunshine, all dressed in blinding white, head to toe. After the first few shots, his confidence returned. He knew that one of these images would soon be on his mother's living room wall amongst all the others that proved they were a model Mormon family.

Afterward, the white temple clothes replaced by Sunday suits and pastel dresses, they all drove two hours north to their hometown, where the reception would be held at the patio and gardens behind the local church. This was the bigger photography challenge: getting good, posed shots of the bride and groom, their rings, their parents and best man and maid of honor, getting good "candids" of everybody there, capturing the right moments at the cutting of the cake, the dance, the tossing of the bouquet. He was grateful for his youngest sister helping his wife mind the two children, because he was completely consumed with his job.

Something invisible happened. The weight and shape and controls of camera and lens were as familiar to his hands as was his own face. The rectangular frame of the viewfinder became his whole world, and through selection and proportion made everything sublime. His sister smiling in her lavender gown and swooping white hat was beautiful, and he told her so. The slant of late afternoon light played on all the lovely faces, and as it faded, he adjusted his exposures, moving in harmony with whatever happened. He was one with his art, utterly free. He had never had any interest in shooting weddings, but this was all good, more than good. He was calmly confident that he was getting the images he wanted: well-framed, properly exposed, decisive moments, a better-than-accurate record of a once-in-a-lifetime day.

And then it was over. The invisible thing that had happened was the planting, just beneath the surface of his awareness, of a seed. A seed of discontent.

Now, as they fly toward home, and toward the job in a cubicle to which he will return tomorrow morning, the job about which he has told himself lies, he gazes at his little family, the family that could not be more perfect, and he smiles. He smiles because he is certain that nothing in this picture will ever change.

F.3 Whose Dream is This, Anyway?

I AM A SPECTATOR along with shadowy others, watching two women playing cards in a New Orleans brothel. They are middle-aged mothers wearing modest dresses, and the card game they are playing is called "Sunset." But as I watch and listen, I realize it's actually "Son-set," played for the purpose of deciding whose son is whose. It seems this game will go on indefinitely, without a winner or loser. The women are cheerful, chatting as they exchange cards. The brothel changes to an underground bunker and the tinny piano music in the background becomes muted machine gun fire. Or are we in the hold of a boat and the sounds outside are the crashing of waves? I don't recognize either of these women. Whose dream is this, anyway?

To Whom It May Concern (A Handwritten Note)

IT APPEARS THAT I may never finish this little book. Of course, nothing is ever finished anyway, there's always more story to tell.

Please do not think unkindly of me, my bad decisions, my falseness. Believe me, I tried to stop it, this mad dictation. To become a carpenter, a fisherman, anything...to transform myself more deeply than just by name. But it was no use, the compulsion ruled, the entanglement reigned. Even here, in my quiet bungalow shaded by palms, with the breeze off the Gulf occasionally lifting the wet blanket of air, and with my gin and tonics leaving perpetual rings on my pages...even here, I couldn't dodge the influx, the dive-bombing stream of language targeted on my cerebral cortex. The words, the voices, the images, they just wouldn't leave me alone.

All these last years of hiding out in this sweet little town surely should have healed me, but no. I needed some deeper source of energy, some sort of inner wellspring from which to derive the clarity of thought, the strength of will, to grow.

I didn't have what it takes. I needed a soul.

Now, I'm exhausted. I feel old, like I've lived too many lives. There's a hurricane coming, with a name that seduces me: Katrina. Evacuation has been ordered, but I'm staying.

—B. R.

Bay St. Louis, Mississippi

August 28, 2005

Part II:

What Happened Next

Amateur Detective

THE ORPHANED MANUSCRIPT HAD arrived at my doorstep by US Mail, clearly sent to me by mistake, but with no return address. It sat on an end-table next to my sofa for a couple of weeks, through the chaos of Christmas with my wife and our young daughter, until I found a few empty hours. It was New Year's Day, 2006. With a cozy fire in the woodstove, I sat in my living room and read the manuscript straight through, and when I turned over the final page I didn't move, just stared at the wall. I had already seen the handwritten note addressed "To whom it may concern." Had the author died in the winds or floods at the epicenter of Katrina? Was I holding someone's last words, their final legacy left to the world? I didn't know what to make of this story, the whole twisted thing, with its sly way of undermining the very notion of authorship itself. Were there two authors as it seemed to suggest, or only one? Where do stories come from, anyway? Who owns them?

Was this story someone's way of coming to terms with a failed marriage, loss of parents, loss of faith? Or even with dissociative identity disorder or schizophrenia? Or was it all just made-up stuff, completely imaginary? It appeared to be a complex combination of memoir and fiction, the mundane and the fanciful, tangling together strands of relationship, philosophy, science, mysticism. ..what else? Most likely, it was a novel in progress. Someone had made a serious effort; they or their heirs deserved to have this printout. I couldn't assume there was an original computer file still existing, given the devastation along the Mississippi coast. It seemed to be my duty to get this stack of papers to its rightful owner.

That was over seven years ago. For more than three of those years, I was a man obsessed. My schedule is pretty full, but whatever free time I could find I devoted to the search for the story's owner. Like A.J. in the manuscript, I had to find out: who is the author? Were these characters, A.J. Campbell and Brandt Robaczynski, real people? Were they just two sides of one person? Was Brett Robinson actually the author's name, or was it a pseudonym? I set out "sleuthing," just like A.J. but with the advantage of a dozen years of technological innovation. I googled every name in the book, starting with the "author," then following up via emails and phone calls the few leads that arose.

Brett Robinson is apparently a common name; searching it gave me businessmen, athletes, newborns, obituaries. My follow-ups, besides being apparently an unforgivable annoyance, were fruitless.

One of the many A.J. Campbells I discovered was an author of books about fishing. And I found it interesting that there was a photographer named A.J. Campbell who had achieved a degree of fame—but that was in Australia, a hundred years ago. Another find was a bit troubling: A.J. Campbell, Junior and Senior, were the names of a missing baby boy and his father, a man who committed suicide. This occurred in Texas in 1958. The baby is believed to have been murdered, but the case remains open. I spent hours but could find no connection to the character in the manuscript.

Robbie Brand was apparently the name of a well-known race car driver, but I found no evidence that he may also have been a fiction writer. Same for the various Robert Brands worldwide.

I also went to the library in my small town—Woodstock, New York—and used the Reader's Guide to Periodical Literature to search for the literary journals named in the story. No luck; apparently, they were all fictitious. I drove to New Jersey and walked the streets of both Sparta and Newton, asking people about the Campbell and Robaczynski families. I inquired at both town offices but accomplished nothing more than raising suspicion about my motives. "Big Bill," the owner of Campbell's Small Engine Sales and Service told me unequivocally that no such Campbell family as the one in the manuscript had ever existed in Sussex County. About Robaczynski...not a trace.

I even made a visit to the Tunnel Diner in Jersey City, just in time. It closed a few weeks later and was fenced in, scheduled for demolition in the shiny refurbishment that was sweeping the waterfront of that once-rough old city. Nobody there had ever heard of a waitress named Felicity from years ago. The place looked tired.

Of course, I checked lists of Katrina casualties on the Internet, but I also went further than that. On the annual trips to New Orleans that I make with my artist wife to sell her fantastical creations at the Mardi Gras Mask Market, I was able to stop in Bay St. Louis, Mississippi and make inquiries: town hall, county tax office, police department, real estate agencies, local merchants.

There were no records for Brett Robinson, Brandt Robaczynski, nor any other name in the manuscript. None of them could be found among the Katrina dead: the 24 in Bay St. Louis, the 51 in Hancock County, the 236 in all of Mississippi, nor the 1,170 in Louisiana. The same was true for hospital records. But did that mean "B.R." was a fiction?

The flagrant corruption and incompetence surrounding the response to Katrina were well documented. People in hospitals were lost when FEMA workers changed the hospital ID bracelets. Politics, bureaucracy, and commercial interests caused deadly delays. Actual help and supplies were prevented from reaching victims. Government squabbles with the third-party disaster-recovery contractor, whose parent company's CEO was friends with President Bush, resulted in confusion about the retrieval and identification of the dead.

My thoughts were just like A.J.'s in the beginning of the book: when it comes to government and politics, *"Everybody's lying, that's who."* How can the truth be found? You dig until you can dig no further. You use your best judgment to sort through the evidence, accepting no media story without solid corroboration—always asking, "if I'm being told this, who is telling me and why do they want me to know it?" You look behind every curtain for the little man at the controls. And even then, you're often left with nothing to lean on but your own intuition.

So...none of my detective efforts produced any valid results whatsoever. Still, the story's characters and its mystery author lurked at the edge of my awareness every day and appeared in my dreams at night. As if they were actual people I'd met, they influenced me, turning my life in new directions: I began reading books I'd never read and researching science and philosophy I'd never studied before. If it was referenced in the manuscript, I dug into it. I found I loved the fiction of Borges and Auster, felt inspired by ancient myths I'd missed in school, was attracted to Talbot's holographic speculations, and was fascinated but flummoxed by the intense quantum theories of Bohm and the kind of mathematics that verged on metaphysics. Those readings led me to others—I struggled to follow Hugh Everett's "many worlds" logic and Schrödinger's thought experiment about the poor cat in a box—and soon I began to feel more educated than I'd ever felt in college all those decades past.

But my distraction was threatening my marriage. And my marriage was more important.

Wendy and I had met in New York City in the nineties. In fact, I had been delightfully grabbed in the early pages of the manuscript by the description of A.J. walking through the Upper West Side. That would have happened just a few blocks from where I was living at the time, and in the same month, same year, and same neighborhood where I met Wendy. She had lived in Queens and Manhattan before moving to Woodstock, and during the nineties she would regularly drive back down to the city to exhibit in an art fair that filled the wide sidewalk of Columbus Avenue from 77th to 81st Streets along the west side of the Natural History Museum. Her canopy was circus-striped yellow and blue in contrast with all the white roofs of the other artists.

I was on my way down Columbus, taking quick looks at the art on either side of me as I wove through the crowd. The tall willowy blonde under the circus tent caught my eye. Wendy was helping a customer, tying on a colorful mask behind the girl's head, when she looked up. We locked eyes and she gave me a brilliant smile. I was stunned but managed a return smile as I kept on walking.

Now I was glancing at art and sidestepping shoppers without really seeing any of it—her face filled my vision. I made my way down to the schoolyard on 77th where there was always a flea market and farmer's market on weekends. I picked up a few vegetables, I distractedly perused the vintage stuff, and then I made a decision. I strode back up Columbus directly to Wendy's booth.

Between customers, our conversation was easy, wandering across music, books, work, family. The lettuce in my bag wilted but I didn't care. Two hours went by, and she needed to wrap up and go home, so I walked in a daze back uptown to my apartment. Over the next weeks, we had long phone conversations, then I visited her in Woodstock. Our connection was powerful, but she had to take some time for the residue of former relationships to fade away. I was alone and unencumbered, eager to dive into love, but recognized the wisdom of taking it slow. I would do anything for her; I had never felt this way before. It stayed a long-distance friendship for three months, but then blessed Eros intervened and said, "Get on with it!" Before long, we lived together in the woods of Willow, outside Woodstock. Five years later, we were married. Five years after that, we had a child.

Over the decades, Wendy and I have had our conflicts, of course—infrequent but always painful. I did not want to be the cause of any more of those. At least that's what I told myself.

One day I was lying on the living room couch with my eyes closed, pondering the Paul Auster novella I had just read, in which there was a fictional character named Paul Auster. I was thinking that this metafictional twinning, a type of mirror that crossed dimensions, may be what was going on in the mystery manuscript. Of the many names in the book, which one might be the actual author?

Wendy was puttering around the kitchen, out of sight but within earshot, while she chatted on the phone with her friend Carolyn. She probably thought I was napping.

I heard her say, "You mean, why did I choose to make masks?"

Then she went on: "Well, I used to say that I didn't know—that I was just fascinated by a display of ceramic masks I once saw in a gallery. But now, I can go a little deeper...."

I could only hear Wendy's side of the conversation, but it said a lot.

"I've told you about my parents, how different they were, how each of their houses, as I went back and forth, had its own brand of insanity....

"Right, so my constant state, in order to feel loved—to survive, actually—was to put on a mask. To be the person they each needed me to be, I switched masks, back and forth. My authentic self was unacceptable, so she had to stay hidden, and that became normal....

"Yeah, so it's no surprise that, as an adult, something in me responded to the idea of masks. And making them became my main creative expression, my income, even my identity....

"Yes, exactly—mask-making became my mask, but it was a necessary mask. It gave me my life....

"Well, these days I try to remember the mythic sense: I am my own wounded healer. My injury is my salvation."

The conversation went on, but I stopped listening. I fell into a reverie about dysfunctional families.... But mostly about A.J. Campbell's discovery of the rage that was in him from infancy, and about his insight that acceptance without action was his way forward. Somehow, Gilberto Cineza had helped him come to that realization. I replayed the scene in my mind.

Then I was startled by the clunk of our front door closing. I got up and went to the window. Wendy was getting in her car. I knew she was on her way to pick up our daughter from a friend's house and go swimming at our favorite spot in the Beaverkill creek, a few miles away. I hadn't been invited.

That's when awareness washed over me like a wave: I could lose my family. As I stood by the window and watched Wendy drive away, I remembered too many times when I had declined to join either her alone or the two of them, for shopping trips, for outings with friends, even for play at home: board games or frisbee or general silliness. I was always too busy with my literary sleuth life. Wendy had protested a few times, but then—I saw it now—she had begun to pull away. I had been only dimly aware of the strained distance between us, and how it was growing. We hadn't made love or even been out on a date for many weeks. She must have been hiding a lot of sadness. What was I doing?

Just a moment earlier when I had overheard Wendy talking about the pain of her childhood, her way of compensating for it, her life's direction...instead of holding her in my thoughts, I had gone immediately to my addiction—yes, that's what it was—my addiction to something utterly irrelevant.

Clearly, she felt abandoned. And our daughter must have felt it as well. How could they not? With my corporate job occupying the weekdays and my three-year obsession stealing my evenings and weekends, they were all alone.

Fuck me! Enough! I drove directly to the swimming hole and joined them.

So, the decision was made. It was time to give up the amateur detective work. I could continue the reading and learning, but the search for someone who couldn't be found had to stop. The price was too high. I hid the stack of pages in a box on a high shelf in my home office and marked the moment with a little internal ceremony of surrender. I visualized letting it all go.

As the months passed, the characters in the story faded into the background of my life, almost gone, but occasionally whispering in my ear. I resisted all their beckonings.

A New Friend

A YEAR WENT BY, and it seemed that the whole episode was finally behind me. Of course, that's when it all changed.

I'm an occasional collector of fine art photographs, and one Friday in May of 2010, I was visiting my friend who runs the Center for Photography at Woodstock, sitting in his office browsing catalogs from past exhibits. We were chatting about the weather as I leafed through pages and glanced at photos. A bold color shot caught my eye with its powerful diagonals. A throng of shouting anti-war marchers, arms in the air, were led by a young woman with a garish sign on a tilting pole: *Desert Storm = Mass Murder!*

The image itself was strong enough to get my attention, but what I saw next took my breath away. In small type below the image was the photographer's name: Campbell James Angus.

I feigned nonchalance. "Who's this guy, Campbell James Angus?"

"Yeah, that's a dramatic shot, isn't it? C.J. Angus. He lives right here in town."

"No way."

"Sure. You thinking about buying that image?"

"No, not really, but the name is familiar. Do you know him? Maybe you could introduce us?"

"I don't know him well, but I know he walks his dog on the Comeau trail every Saturday morning, winter and summer. I've seen him there a couple of times."

I thanked him, said my goodbyes, and wrestled my excitement the whole eight-mile drive home. Was it possible that this guy C.J. Angus, uncannily similar in name and a photographer no less, was the character in my mystery manuscript? Or maybe even its author?

The next morning was fresh and cool, promising one of those perfect spring days that made me love the Catskills. I surprised Wendy by volunteering to take our friendly houndish mutt Casper for a walk and I headed to the Comeau property, a beautiful patch of woods and fields surrounding the Woodstock town offices.

It was all absurdly easy. Standing at the edge of a meadow watching their unleashed dogs romp in the tall grass were a man and a woman. The man had a digital SLR slung around his shoulder; it had to be him. I unclipped Casper, who bounded with joy into the dog party as I said hello and joined the human chat: all dog talk, of course. It was only a few minutes before the woman whistled her Shepherd over, said "Gotta go," and was gone.

The man turned to me. "C.J.," he said, and held out his hand. I shook it, told him my name, and he said, "I was just going to walk the trail with Bodhi; do you and Casper wanna come along?" We headed for the shady path that meandered through the forest, his barrel-chested black Lab and my slender tan hound bounding ahead, criss-crossing, scuffling over a stick with fierce, happy growls.

C.J. Angus was younger and taller than me, his close-cropped hair blonde going gray. When he lifted his baseball cap that read "French Quarter," I saw he was entirely bald on top. His face and hands were narrow and pale, but strong-looking. He had a sincerity of manner that was almost naïve but not quite, and I liked the directness of his gaze.

I had already decided that I would try to get to know C.J. first, before I said anything about the manuscript. It was not difficult. We talked while we strolled the root-clogged trail along the creek, the Sawkill, that swirled around boulders and pooled in sun-dappled shade. I learned that he had indeed been making his living for nearly two decades as a photographer and videographer—a tougher challenge upstate than it was during his many years in the city, but worth it for the more relaxed lifestyle, he said. He had two adult kids from his first marriage, both in New Jersey. Now he lived with his second wife Denise, a real estate agent who occasionally did freelance curating work for regional galleries and museums. He was originally from rural Utah, a Mormon boy who left the religion behind.

I kept a poker face, traded equivalent information about myself, but inside was breathlessly checking off the synchronicities, one by one.

As we walked our now leashed dogs to the parking lot, I told him I occasionally buy photographic art and I'd be interested to see his work. This contained a thread of truth but was mostly a ruse intended to get more information. He said he had a couple of immediate errands to run but I could come by his house mid-afternoon and look through some images. Our dogs hopped into our respective cars and we went our separate ways.

I didn't feel good about being disingenuous with my new friend, and I wasn't sure what I'd say to him next. I was just driving blind here. I went home and pulled the manuscript off the shelf. An hour ahead of time, I drove into town, stopped at Catskill Art and Office Supply, and stood by their Xerox copier while the stack of pages chunked one by one through the machine.

C.J.'s house was on the oddest-named street in Woodstock, Hill 99. It was a modest fifties ranch that had sprawled a bit with add-ons, all shaded by a stand of tall old pines. The inside was cool and dark, with a cozy, welcoming feeling. I saw a mounted photo of a desert scene on one wall, and on another was a framed poster of the famous Milton Glaser illustration of Bob Dylan in profile, his hair in psychedelic colors. This could be another link to the book, but not a strong one; a Dylan fan in Woodstock is nothing unique.

C.J. led me into a wing that seemed to have once been a garage but was now a windowless studio with recessed lighting, all warm tones, oak shelves lining the walls, and a wide counter crowned with an assortment of gleaming hardware, most of it sporting the Apple logo.

I had left the manuscript in the car, wanting to be absolutely sure before leaping into that strange territory. But I didn't know what would make me sure.

When we entered the room, music was playing, and it was definitely not Dylan. It was a dark, slow jazz song with an androgynous vocal, a liquid tenor, almost falsetto, wavering long on every phrase: "What is your frequency...you who tell lies to me...with such impunity...and no remorse...where do you broadcast from...what wavelength are you on...are you like me?" The music was hypnotic, and I had to resist its spooky magnetism so I could pay attention to the oversized binder C.J. had pulled from a shelf. "This is some of my old work on film," he was saying. "Not all of it is digitized yet, but I'm working through it."

He turned pages slowly as I watched with glazed eyes. The song ended and a new one began: "It's four o'clock in the morning...on a moonless Monday night...there's nobody left on the street...not a thing's even movin'...except the lonely traffic light...and a man who appears mysteriously...he only looks a lot like me...."

I had to interrupt C.J.. "What is this music?" He reached over to the CD player and handed me the jewel case: *Don't Just Dance* by Eric Wood. The little hairs stood up on the back of my neck. I looked at the CD shelf and saw Eric Wood's name on two more spines: *Letters from the Earth* and *Illustrated Night*.

An artist this obscure...it had to be the final coincidence. Now was the time for the truth.

"Hey C.J.," I said, "I have to make a confession. I am interested in your photography, but that's not why I came here today."

His stare pierced me for a long moment. "What d'you mean?" he said, in a low, flat tone.

"I already knew who you were when we met this morning." The CD reached its end, and the room went silent except for my voice. He listened stony-faced as I stumbled through an embarrassed explanation of how I got his name from my friend at CPW and was gathering information throughout our walk at the Comeau, like some kind of stalker. He closed the binder with a quick motion. I had to get to the point before he kicked me out of his house.

"All of this is because of something that arrived in my mailbox, totally by mistake, several years ago: a manuscript of a novel or memoir or something, a book with a character in it that seems to be you. I've been searching for the author, and now I think maybe this book is yours."

C.J. kept staring at me. He didn't smile. "That sounds pretty damned crazy, you know."

"So you haven't written a book about yourself and...other people, other stuff?"

"No, I'm not a writer, never was. And right now I'm thinking, 'what is this bullshit, is this guy a scam artist of some kind?' So really, you need to explain yourself now."

"OK...I can't really explain. If you didn't write it, then it must have been a friend of yours or something. The author's name on the first page doesn't lead anywhere." I was afraid to tell him the author's name; it was too much like mine.

He turned his back to me and put the binder into its slot on the shelf. When he faced me, his voice had an edge. "Why the hell does any of this matter?"

"I wanna give you a copy of the manuscript. If you read it, you'll see why it matters, I promise. Look, I'm sorry about all this weirdness after we just met, but trust me, really. Take a couple of hours and read it, then we'll get together again and talk."

"Hmm. Maybe, maybe not." He still looked stern, then he shrugged. "OK, give me the thing, I'll take a look."

DURING THE NEXT FEW days, I convinced myself that nothing would come of all this. Surely it was just a crazy bit of luck that someone had invented a fictional story and just happened to choose a name, occupation, origins, and musical tastes that matched up with a real person. After all, there were billions of people in the world, millions just in New York City. Numerical odds demand some coincidence. So C.J. and I would just have a laugh about it, and it would all fade into the past.

The following Thursday night, I got a call from C.J. He did not sound friendly as he said, "I want to head you off so you don't just show up at the Comeau and crash my dog walk again. Let's meet on Friday afternoon at Joshua's, upstairs in the coffee bar. We have some talking to do."

I PARKED IN WOODSTOCK'S small municipal lot behind the building where Wendy had her studio and small showroom. She was on the third floor in the only three-story building in town. A unique vision and skillful hands had created a real livelihood, an unusual feat for any artist, but even more so for a maker of masks. Her colorful, fanciful, elegant creations appealed to a narrow niche of buyers, but those people did manage to find her. She knew I was meeting with C.J. today; I had told her everything that was going on, doing my best to be transparent, lest my addiction get between us again.

My route took me down Tinker Street past the colorful little assembly of businesses that gave Woodstock some of its destination status—bookstore, gift shops, taco and ice-cream joint, lingerie store, art gallery—to the corner restaurant and its heavy, dark-wood door with its round window and Mediterranean accents. I took a deep breath of delicious coffee aroma as I reached the top of the narrow stairs to Joshua's Java Lounge, a sunlit room overlooking Tinker Street. Through the opposite window, I could see the building where Bob Dylan wrote many songs back in 1964, when it was the Café Espresso. Now it was the photography center where I had stumbled upon C.J.'s photo.

C.J. was already there, the stack of pages on the table in front of him. Without a hello, he launched in, his finger poking the paper: "OK, first, look at the name right here on the first page. That's *you*, right?" I was already shaking my head no, but he didn't pause. "So why the lying? But even worse," and here his voice dropped down to a hoarse, menacing whisper, "how the fuck did you get all this information about me?" His eyes looked a little wild and suddenly it hit me in the gut—not just in my head this time—how truly creepy this must feel to him. Just as it already had, to that other version of himself, hidden in the pages on the table in front of him. But I had to defend myself first.

"No," I said, "that is not my name on the first page. It is similar to my name, and that must be why it was mailed to me."

"Why should I believe you?" His voice was low but harsh, his eyes fierce. He scared me.

"I have nothing to gain here," I said, hoping for a balance of kindness and firmness. "I absolutely did not write this and I don't know who did. I am not playing any kind of trick on you. But if it really is about your life, and you don't know who wrote it either, then it's freaking me out, too."

He leaned his head in his hands and groaned as if he were suddenly overcome with fatigue. "It's been like some kind of fucked-up nightmare these last few days. I called my ex-wife and several friends, made accusations, got in arguments over the phone, just being stupid and reactionary. I'm not usually that rash. And all along I knew that some of the stuff in here could not have been written by any of them anyway. It was strictly private."

He looked up at me and I nodded. We both knew what I voiced next: "Just like the character A.J. in the story. It's like you're repeating history."

"Yeah, just like that. But no, not exactly." He tapped the manuscript with a finger. "Things that happened to him in here didn't happen to me back then. I mean, I didn't find published stories like he did. That's what's happening to me *now*. In reality."

"Right, but all the other stuff—"

"No, no, it's hard to explain. There's a lot of this book that's just not true, not even close. But at the same time, it's *all* true at sort of a deeper level, if you know what I mean."

"Um...I'm not sure...."

"Sort of symbolically, or like a theme in my life, my own struggles.... Ah, fuck it, never mind." He sat up straighter, suddenly agitated. "See, the real problem is, there are just too goddamn many things, I mean private shit, precise details, my personal history, that *are* totally true. It's just fucking impossible!"

We sat silent for a moment, each of us wrapped in our own thoughts. He was scowling and his fingers drummed the table. The leaves of the big sycamore outside the windows quivered in the sunshine. I said, "You want a coffee or something? I'll buy."

"No," he said. I went to the bar and ordered an iced coffee, treated it with milk and sugar, and brought it back to the table. He had not moved. He still frowned at the tabletop.

"Well," I said as I sat down, "we haven't talked yet about the other characters in the book, especially the college kid. What about him?"

"Who the hell knows? He's not my concern. Probably just fiction, a web of lies."

I took a long sip. "My theory is that he's the author, a fictionalized version. I searched the various names he used, and the other people's too. Nothing. I mean, maybe some private investigator could find a better lead, but I don't have the budget for that."

His eyes blazed at me again and the knife-edge returned to his voice. "Look, here's what I want to do. I want you to make no more copies of the manuscript, and I want you to give the original to me."

"Wait...why would I do that? This thing was mailed to me."

"OK, well...I'm done. I've had enough." He beckoned to a bulky guy who'd been sitting at another table reading a newspaper. I'd noticed him earlier because it's rare to see a necktie in Woodstock.

C.J. leaned back in his chair and pointed his finger at me. "Not only are you lying, but now you're even shaking me down for money to do some bullshit investigation."

"What? No, I'm not—" The guy with the tie had gotten up and was now at our table, standing over me.

C.J. said, "This is Frank. He's my lawyer. Frank, say your piece."

I was speechless. I looked at C.J. then up at Frank, who stared down at me. He spoke in a pleasant but firm tone. "Mr. Robison, this is an informal request at this point. You need to cease and desist any activity related to the manuscript in your possession. To make it public in any way, or to share it with any other person, would constitute invasion of privacy, defamation of character, and also violation of copyright regarding some of the content in the manuscript."

"Wow. Is this a joke?"

"No joke," C.J. said.

"But I have no ulterior motives here at all. I just wanted to solve a mystery, not to harm you in any way." There was too much whine in my protest.

C.J. just looked at me. Frank spoke: "That's all we have to say, Mr. Robison. Don't pursue this, or I'll have to take a more formal position."

C.J. grabbed the manuscript copy and stood up. I followed. "What the fuck! Why are you so threatened? Your actual name is not even in the—."

Frank glared at me and shook his head no. Then he turned his back and he and C.J. were both down the stairs and gone. I glanced around; what a goddamned humiliating scene. Most people kept their eyes down, but the scraggly-bearded barista smirked at me. I left my coffee on the table and went home.

No Answers

So that was the end of my new friendship and the final nail in the coffin of my investigation into the mystery manuscript. I put it back on its shelf in a box. In subsequent months I occasionally saw C.J. in town, browsing the Saturday flea market or having coffee at an outdoor table. He was usually with his wife, and I can only assume he saw me too, but we avoided any contact.

I had submitted to his demand to stop pursuing the mystery, but my mind wouldn't let go of what had happened. I kept gnawing on it like a dog on a bone. For weeks, I thought about it from every angle.

Are his legal threats valid? Do I need to defend myself? I don't like lawyers and don't want to spend money to find out what my rights are. This manuscript thing isn't worth it; it's just a...a hobby. I can give it up.

But why did C.J. respond in such a hostile way? Is he hiding something? What? There's no crime in the story, but there are certainly some things that could be embarrassing. Maybe they're secrets he's keeping from someone. Is he under pressure from his wife or ex-wife?

Or is it all just because he's very sensitive about privacy?

He could have simply claimed to be the author and asked for the original manuscript. I probably would have believed him and surrendered it, glad to solve the mystery. He didn't do that; why not? The answer that feels right: because he is not the author, and he is an honest guy.

Or is it all a pose? Is he actually the author but would rather put on this tough-guy act than claim the book? Why? That would be like wearing a mask over a mask. It doesn't feel true, but...if he isn't the author, who is? I'm back to the same question.

Could it be a type of forgery, sent from Mississippi as a sub-terfuge? Let's say C.J. had a close friend to whom he told his secrets. Then he had a falling out with that friend, who is now trying to hurt him by spreading the information. In that case, the former friend could have easily published the material on the web, so that doesn't make sense. Instead, the person sent it to me, in the same town where C.J. lives, counting on me to pass it along to him. And why, instead of just laying out all the naked secrets, did the author change it into this fancy novel-type thing with circuitous plotlines and metaphor and additional characters? These are all masks.

So maybe it's a form of "gaslighting," a way to get revenge by making him feel like he's going crazy. Like what that deliciously oily Charles Boyer did to sweet Ingrid Bergman in the classic 1944 movie: secretly dimming the gaslights, moving a picture, stealing a brooch, but telling her it's all in her head, driving her mad for his own evil ends. It's an awful lot of trouble to go to...which makes it all the more nasty.

What if it's me who's being gaslighted? But why? Is this some sort of con and I'm the mark? If it were, I would have been asked for something, which I have not.

Occam's Razor states that, all things being equal, the simplest answer is most likely true. The simplest answer: C.J. is an honest guy who doesn't know how this betrayal happened, but he just doesn't want his insecurities, mistakes, relationships, struggles—all the things that make up a private life—exposed to the world. What's wrong with that? I would do the same thing in his shoes.

And I had to acknowledge that I was grateful I *wasn't* in his shoes, that I was just a bystander. What happened to him had not happened to me.

So, after all the obsessive analysis, the bottom line was that I discovered I had empathy for him. I understood. But still, I was frustrated; I was in a straitjacket; I couldn't do anything with the manuscript, not even show it to people, without causing myself legal trouble. That's why I put it on the shelf. Again. But now, it was an even bigger mystery than before: a real object of unknown origin, suddenly being treated as if it didn't exist.

It was like those giant skeletons I had read about. In the late 1800s and early 1900s there were hundreds of news stories across the country about discoveries by many people, farmers to archaeologists, of skeletons that were eight feet tall and more. Even a well-documented 1894 Smithsonian excavation of burial mounds in West Virginia reported abnormally tall skeletons. What happened to the physical evidence? Today this information is treated as if it never existed, denied rather than investigated, too threatening to our tame consensual worldview.

Would the orphaned manuscript be just another buried story, another cover-up that never, so to speak, makes the history books? Even if C.J. preferred to deny the mystery, at least I knew of its existence. I had no answers, but the question itself was a crowbar prying open my skull: How did this happen? Who is the author?

And why me? How was I chosen to be the rat in this maze? Who is the experimenter? My new-age friends might suggest there is a lesson for me to learn, that I had somehow attracted this puzzle into my life as a stepping stone toward higher awareness. Puzzle... conundrum... enigma. Some might say a "closed book." Just like life. The whole damned adventure is a puzzle—and not every puzzle has a solution. Perhaps the best thing I can learn here is to not let it eat me up. Relax into the mystery. Embrace the enigma. Yeah, that's it.

Maybe I'll sing along with Paul (leaving the Mother Mary part out): *Let it be, just let it be.*

Masks and Circles

THE SUMMER OF 2010 stretched on. During that time, I told Wendy about what had happened with C.J., and my thoughts about it all. Of course, she was already thoroughly familiar with my pursuit of the manuscript's author, but she still hadn't read it. I went along with her suggestion to give C.J. some space, not invade his privacy further, even stay away from the Comeau property on Saturday mornings.

I usually follow Wendy's advice, because she is wise.

One cool morning after a rain we were walking our dog on a circular trail through the woods around the Catskills Interpretive Center. The trail was like a tunnel through a rainforest, everything green and dripping and draped with vines. We were talking about a subject she had been studying—Anima/Animus, Self, Persona, Shadow, the primary Jungian archetypes—when, after a lag in the conversation, she said, "The word 'I' is a mask."

I said, "As in Jung's idea of Persona?"

"Not exactly. It's more than our social masks, I think. Maybe Jung never pinned down the borderline between Persona and Self. 'I' is sort of both, and neither."

I said, "Hmm. But a mask? You mean, right now, if I say, 'I am hungry,' I'm somehow dishonest?"

"Are you hungry?"

"Yes, but that's not the point."

"Casper!" she blurted. The dog was pulling her faster than she wanted to walk. She unclipped the leash from his collar, and he trotted forward on the trail, nose to the ground. A free dog...against the rules on this trail.

"I know," she said when I raised an eyebrow. "If they don't see him, it's all good."

"Outlaw."

"So anyway, there's nothing dishonest about a mask," she said as she coiled up the leash. "Don't think of it as...deception. It's simply a human condition. What I meant was, to speak 'I,' or possibly even more so, to *write* 'I,' is to imagine a self as if it exists as a unique thing in that moment. It's like trying to stop a river. A photograph of a river is not the river."

"Okay. Well, forgive the obsession, but that makes me think of the manuscript. I can see there are masks everywhere." I batted away a mosquito near my ear, and I heard annoyance in my voice. "But who is the 'I' in it? Or the several 'I's?"

She laughed. "Well, that's what I was thinking about too. The stuff you've told me from the book raises the old question I've had: is there such a thing as a true self, or is it masks all the way down? In the case of that manuscript, I'd say it's mask upon mask upon mask, *ad infinitum*. No face is even there."

"Yikes. Not sure I can grasp that. Casper, come!" I didn't want him getting out of my sight. He ignored me but slowed his pace. "In other words, it's a complete illusion? No author at all? A game of Three-Card Monte played by the universe, and the joke's on me?"

"Maybe. And on C.J."

"Or it's all in my mind. I'm hallucinating. Nutso."

She smiled. "Maybe. But you said 'I,' so who knows?"

"Wonderful."

Then we kept on walking the wooded circle in the fresh morning air, bumping shoulders, holding hands, talking about lucky Casper—aaah, a dog's life, to be fed, sheltered, loved, and never once be concerned with something called "I."

Stop Making Sense

I COULDN'T LET IT be. I was still in the grip of the addiction. I had to explain everything. One thing after another would happen, and I would immediately ask, "What is the story here? Who is writing it? How does it fit into my own story?"

The multinational software company that employs me as an Instructional Designer went through another round of layoffs, a follow-up to the big downsizing that happened after the financial crisis of 2008. I was the only person in my department left standing. There was no more Training Group, so I was offered a job in the Estimation Office—something entirely outside my interest or background. What choice did I have? I took it.

But I had a new way of looking at such events. How does this dramatic twist advance the plot of my life? For whose entertainment? Is this a play in which I am a character—like Macbeth says, "a poor player that struts and frets his hour upon the stage"? If it's "a tale told by an idiot, full of sound and fury, signifying nothing," who is that idiot? Who wrote the script? Of course, Macbeth had much more reason to be pessimistic than I did. Maybe the playwright was not an idiot at all.

In December, Wendy and I took our eight-year-old daughter and went on vacation to Tulum, Mexico. We stayed in an exquisite little tropical hotel nestled in the jungle just across a narrow road from the beach. White sand and pastel stucco striped with palm shadows, thatched roofs and rustic balconies, a laid-back restaurant/bar, perfect sunshine, rolling waves, long-needed relaxation. My two beautiful girls, carefree, laughing and playing. But when we peeled ourselves off the lounge chairs and toured the nearby Mayan ruins, first the Tulum seaport then the inland city of Cobá, I had a different type of experience.

A sublime strangeness filled the air like an exotic perfume, slightly alarming, slightly repugnant, irresistibly alluring. I was fascinated by the humans who had lived in these places over a thousand years ago, who had stacked these stones and carved these glyphs. Their art, architecture, language, games, culture: all so alien. If I could read their stories, would I even recognize my species?

We climbed to the top of Nohoch Mul, the central pyramid of Cobá. We looked out across the jungles of the Yucatan and down on the network of white stone roads built eons ago. I was in a trance of imagination, conjuring a scene so radically different from my everyday reality that, in the end, it left me with one feeling: I was stunned with wonder at the mysterious, majestic complexity of the world.

As I sat on a huge stone step near the top of the pyramid, I overheard the conversation of a man and woman near me.

"You know," he said, "we're only two years away from the end of the Mayan calendar. Meaning the end of the world, of course."

"But that's not what it means," she replied. "The Long Count calendar indicates that in December of 2012, the 13th *baktun*, which means about 394 years, comes to an end. You know, it just rolls over to a row of zeros."

"Like an odometer."

"Yeah. That marks a cycle of about 5,000 years from the beginning of that calendar—but then the 14th *baktun* begins. Not the end of the world."

He laughed. "You sure?"

"Well, I prefer to see it as a point that signals a worldwide shift in consciousness—you know, the dawn of the age of Aquarius."

When he started singing the song from *Hair*, I stopped listening. We are all so thoroughly programmed by our culture, is it even valid to ask whether we own our individual stories?

In early May of 2011, Wendy and I were working on getting our vegetable garden ready for planting, when on the radio came an announcement that Osama bin Laden had been killed and his body "buried at sea."

We both said, "What?" Then we started laughing. "Buried at sea!" Laughter escalating. "Oh, right, buried at sea—sorry, can't look at his body, it's buried at sea!" Whoops and howls. "Out of respect for Muslim tradition, ha!"

I had never heard anything so preposterous. It was amazing that anyone would believe it—but, I reminded myself, the official narrative of what happened on 9/11 was still swallowed by many people. As were the WMD lies, and so much more. Believing the stories that Daddy Government tells you is so much easier than doing any questioning.

Who wrote those stories? But more importantly, who wrote the story of your belief in those stories?

OUR GARDEN GREW. WE had dirt under our fingernails, and we ate healthy organic dinners every night. On our little plot of land cleared from the forests of the Catskill Mountains, shadows of pines moved across day after day, birds flitted and trilled, deer and rabbits grazed. We sat on our deck with cups of tea and watched it all.

The orphaned manuscript hid in darkness in its box, but it still had not left me. The book was the world, the world was the book. Had I been admirably striving to make sense of the universe, or was I an addict in relapse? Because it was part of A.J.'s—or perhaps I should say C.J.'s—story, I had read the Twelve Steps of Alcoholics Anonymous. I knew I had to surrender, to hand over my arrogant and impulsive will to some greater power. I had to stop demanding to know. I had to stop making sense.

Goodbye

In August, when my birthday arrived, I decided to give myself an unusual gift: a day home alone with a hefty dose of magic mushrooms.

Through a friend, I had procured a chocolate bar laced with 'shrooms, and I'd been waiting for the right opportunity. Wendy agreed to take the dog with her and spend a long day in her studio, and our daughter would go after school to a friend's house for a sleepover. I had had experience with psychedelics in the past and didn't feel the need for supervision, but I did pay attention to set and setting. In psychonaut parlance, "set" is the mental state I would bring to the experience, like my thoughts, mood, expectations, even my physical health. Overall, I was feeling strong and positive. That niggling anxiety about the manuscript had begun to fade. "Setting" is the physical and social environment, or in this case, non-social environment. I was at home, nothing threatening, no "trip sitter" needed.

An hour after I ate the chunk of chocolate, I was feeling the expected exhilaration. The forest beyond my deck rail looked exceptionally alive and beautiful in the morning light. Every leaf quivered and sparkled. My back was in full contact with the wicker chair. My feet were bare on the boards. I was happy to be smiling, and smiling because I was happy.

More time passed and I went on several journeys, once to the kitchen for a glass of the best water I'd ever had...once to the lawn where I picked up a fallen stick that said "Y" and tossed it with a beautiful spin through a geometrically perfect arc into the woods while shouting "Y not?"...once to the bathroom where I looked for a long time at my face in the mirror, fascinated by its maskness, knowing that an eye cannot see itself and a reflection is not the truth.

Back at my spot on the deck chair, I chatted aloud with myself:

"What exactly have you been doing?"

"Seeking the author."

"Does every story require an author? Is your life a story?"

"I'd like to think I'm the author of my own story."

"But how do you know that's true?"

"I don't. I just have to act as if it's true."

"How do you know the author you seek even exists?"

"I guess I don't. But the manuscript seems like evidence."

"You mean like the world itself is evidence of a creator?"

"Hmm...I'm not sure that's an accurate analogy. But...maybe."

"What difference does it make whether there is an author or not?"

"It doesn't have to make any difference at all. I can surrender to not knowing, but still have respect for the creation, and be open to whatever new knowledge comes my way."

Sometime later I found myself thinking about the Ray Bradbury book from my teen years, *Fahrenheit 451*, and I was vividly imagining the people hiding in the forest, and how each of them had memorized an entire book—had *become* that book. Then all my recent reading began to rise up like mist from my neurons and synapses. I thought of the Borges story, "The Library of Babel," and it seemed as if I could remember it wholly, every word, and in my mind's eye, with my body's eyes open, I saw in great detail the endless connected hexagons and spiral staircases receding into the distance, the infinitely repeating shelves and identical volumes of 410 pages each, and the pages and pages and pages of alphabetical symbols in every possible combination.

It seemed as if Borges had had his own twisted vision of the Akashic Records—that invisible repository of everything—not Blavatsky's Theosophical version, not Steiner's Anthroposophical version, but his own. Or mine. I saw in faint lines of flowing color a vast web of connections, a Net of Indra with a jewel at every node, and every jewel a library of infinite facets, of infinite stories that were also mirrors reflecting the infinite stories in every other library. Every event, thought, action, emotion, imagination...past, present, future...of all beings, human and other, in all universes everywhere. I sat awestruck as I watched new jewels coming into being, the web forever branching, with each universe born of a new possibility. Everett's many-worlds multiverse, with each world irretrievably separate from every other, so Schrödinger's cat can be both alive and dead, and Bohm's aquarium fish one or many, and all those things that the Photographer and the Writer and their creator the Author of my authorless book liked to prattle on about, and all of it—all of it—recorded here in the great Library.

There it is, in fact! I see it—my authorless book—right there on that shelf in the Library, its spine glowing with the correct jumble of symbols. It can never be lost, it will be there forever, if anyone ever needs it.

Without awareness of moving, I must have gone to the closet and pulled the boxed manuscript down from its actual shelf. Now I was leafing through it, certain that I had every line on every page committed to my own memory, which was also plugged into the Akashic Records, the Library of Babel. This paper artifact made from dead trees was nothing more than a coarse burden, a burlap bag of mud bricks on my spiritual back. The perfect solution was to cause it to disappear from this universe.

I remembered the ritual performed by both Brandt and Felicity. I grinned as I thought this thought, because, after all, they were merely fiction. Or were they? Ha! But I would perform the ritual again, with even deeper significance. I wheeled an old charcoal grill out of the garage into my driveway. I took the manuscript out of its box and put the stack of pages in the charcoal bed. I squirted it with lighter fluid until the paper looked soaked, struck a match, and threw it in. With the whoosh and the blue-orange blaze, I dropped to my knees. A fierce light radiated out from the grill. Involuntarily, my arms flew up, my hands wide, and it was like a white bird leaped from my fingers to the sky. I was certain I heard music but could not be sure what it was. Tympani, perhaps? This was it, really it—the original work, the torturous typescript, the insane story, even the handwritten note, the author's very last trace, the end.

I encouraged its holy burning with more lighter fluid and a stick to stir the pages toward the flames. Edges browned and curled; string after string of black sigils and alien hieroglyphs with magical powers both ominous and comical surrendered meekly to the fiery furnace. Eventually, all that remained was a pile of delicate black flakes in the afternoon sunshine, stirring in a faint breeze. Insignificant. Before Wendy came home that evening, before I returned to normal thought, I had scooped the ashes into the manuscript box, taped it up, and addressed it to C.J. Angus on Hill 99, Woodstock.

The next day I didn't question my intoxicated plan; I dropped the box off at the Post Office. C.J. could have the original, as he demanded—ha!

The orphaned manuscript was gone from my world at last. Who is the author? I'll never know.

An Impossibility

MORE THAN A YEAR passed. On December 21, 2012, the day that media hucksters claimed would be the end of the world predicted by misunderstood Mayan prophecies, I got my first tattoo. I selected that day as a statement against culturally manufactured doom, a gesture of strength. I'm a Leo, so I chose to mark my body with a tribal rendition of a lion's face with a wild mane, all black but for the red dots of the lion's eyes.

A few weeks later, I was at work and got an email from a co-worker who is also a friend. We chat in the break room sometimes, and I had shown her the tattoo on my right forearm. Her email contained photos of the cover of a poetry book, an anthology, and of an inside page that contained a short poem. She wrote, *Congratulations on getting your poem published! Too bad they misspelled your name!*

I wrote back *Thanks, but...*, and informed her that I didn't write the poem, it must be some kind of weird coincidence. I left it at that. The poem made reference to my location, my activities—certainly it seemed to be about me—but I'm not sure she was even aware that the book was published years earlier, in 2009, and the poem written sometime before that.

A hidden person knew me, my mind, my story, even my future. It was an impossibility, of course. But I must say, I wasn't really surprised.

12/21/12

A Poem by Brett Robinson

Ancient prophets in southern jungles
predict an end,
Our 5 millenia, our 13th *baktun*—done.
Media blares: we're futureless.
Despair!

Me, I won't comply.
I'll walk the main street of my small town
whose name brands a generation,
From my wife's shop, maker of masks that tell truth,
Past the faded thrones of graying troubadour gods,
To the tattoo man.
Van's "Listen to the Lion" will ring in my ears
As the needle carves on my forearm
A fierce, regal visage,
A mane windblown and wild.
While liars lie from pulpits

about all that we should fear, and
Signal their virtue, and
Urge our submission, and
Lie, and lie, and lie....

I'll flex that Leo muscle
And laugh.

Acknowledgments

FOR VALUABLE FEEDBACK ON several levels, I'm very grateful to Wendy Drolma, Val Vadeboncoeur, Marta Szabo, Jim Kullander, Tina Klem, Mark Morganstern, and Tom Newton.

For inspiration, good songs, and permission to quote them, I'm grateful to Eric Wood.

For previously publishing parts of this novel, my thanks go to the following journals (which are apparently no longer operational):

- *Literal Latte* for "Desert Vacation" (Short Short Contest Winner)

- *Two Cities Review* for "Another War"

About the Author

BRENT ROBISON LIVES IN the Catskill Mountains of New York with his artist wife. His fiction has appeared in over a dozen literary journals and several anthologies, and has won the *Literal Latte* Short Short Award, the *Chronogram* Short Fiction Contest, a Fiction Fellowship from the New Jersey Council on the Arts, and a Pushcart Prize nomination. His collection of linked short stories, *The Principle of Ultimate Indivisibility*, and his mystery novel, *Ponckhockie Union*, are available from booksellers everywhere.

He blogs occasionally at https://ultimate-indivisibility.com and co-hosts The Strange Recital, https://thestrangerecital.com, a podcast about fiction that questions the nature of reality.

A Request

IF YOU ENJOYED THIS book, its author and publisher would be grateful if you would post a short (or long) review on the website where you bought the book an/or on *goodreads.com* or other book review sites.